Grimgar of Fantasy and Ash

level.11 -
At That Time, We Each Dreamed on Our Own Paths

Written by: Ao Jyumonji
Illustrations by: Eiri Shirai

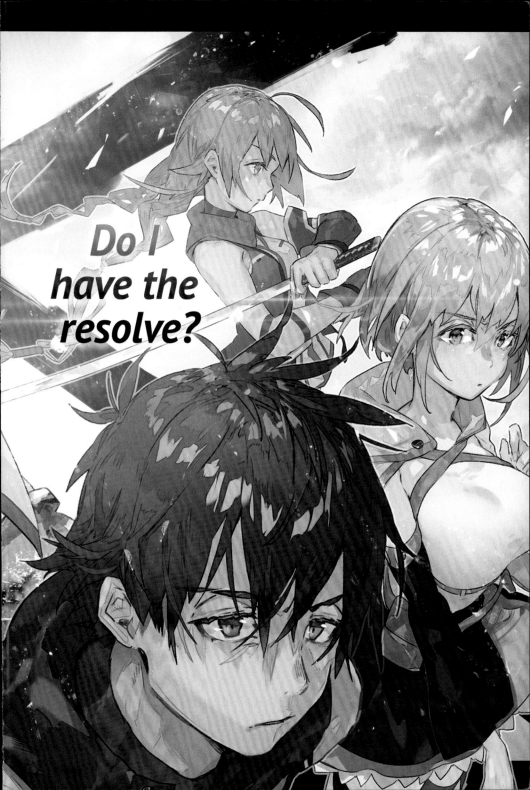

No matter
where I am.
My heart's
on edge.

The flight from Thousand Valley could end at any time.

Grimgar of Fantasy and Ash

GRIMGAR OF FANTASY AND ASH, LEVEL. 11

Copyright © 2017 Ao Jyumonji
Illustrations by Eiri Shirai

First published in Japan in 2017 by
OVERLAP Inc., Ltd., Tokyo.
English translation rights arranged with
OVERLAP Inc., Ltd., Tokyo.

Follow Seven Seas Entertainment online at
sevenseasentertainment.com.
Experience J-Novel Club books online at j-novel.club.

TRANSLATION: Sean McCann
J-NOVEL EDITOR: Emily Sorensen
COVER DESIGN: KC Fabellon
INTERIOR LAYOUT & DESIGN: Clay Gardner
COPY EDITOR: Brian Kearney
PROOFREADER: Christina Lynn
LIGHT NOVEL EDITOR: Nibedita Sen
EDITOR-IN-CHIEF: Adam Arnold
PUBLISHER: Jason DeAngelis

ISBN: 978-1-64275-704-0
Printed in Canada
First Printing: October 2019
10 9 8 7 6 5 4 3 2 1

Grimgar of Fantasy and Ash

level. 11 — At That Time, We Each Dreamed on Our Own Paths

Presented by
AO JYUMONJI

Illustrated by
EIRI SHIRAI

Table of Contents

Grimgar
of
Fantasy and Ash

HE TOOK A DEEP BREATH, then exhaled.

It seemed that, for a while, he'd forgotten to breathe.

A while?

How long was a while?

He didn't know. The noise—

There were noises off in the distance. An awful lot of different ones.

The distance?

No, maybe that wasn't it. The noises might be echoing inside his head. Deep inside. If so, they weren't far off at all. It was the opposite. They were close. Very close.

So very close that, as a result, he couldn't hear them?

His hands were on the ground.

Where was this again?

Not outside. Indoors. But the ground wasn't covered. It was a dirt floor.

Her face was between his hands. Why was it like this? Even as he wondered that, he had no idea, but from where he was looking down on her from a position like he had stopped in the middle of a push-up, he could see that her eyes were almost closed, and her lips slightly parted. Like her whole body was limp.

Despite that, if he were to talk to her, it felt like she'd respond. So why didn't he? It was such a simple thing. He had only to call her name, that was all, and yet for some reason he couldn't do it.

Why?

Am I...scared?

But scared of what?

I don't understand it. I don't know.

I'm not going to understand anyway, so maybe things are fine this way. Yeah.

Things are fine this way.

I'll leave her be. That's for the best. Yeah. That's what I'll do.

How did things turn out like this? It doesn't matter. Get your act together. You're the leader, aren't you? Not much of one, but the leader nonetheless. This is no time for spacing out. Don't think about anything unnecessary. Right now, there must be things you ought to be doing. Do them. If you have time to think, use it to do them.

He stood up and looked to the entrance. Shihoru was sitting with her back leaned against the bars to his left. Her eyes were wide, her teeth gritted, and her jaw trembling as she looked at him.

Shihoru tried to say something. But her voice didn't seem to come out.

Haruhiro cocked his head to the side. What could it be?

Shihoru had an incredible look on her face. Like she had just witnessed something terrible.

"It's okay," he said to Shihoru and smiled. Then Haruhiro breathed out.

It was okay. Everything was okay.

Okay.

Okay.

Okay.

No, wait. Now wasn't the time to be saying things were okay. He had things he needed to do.

Come to think of it, where was his stiletto?

Oh.

Right next to him.

When he tried to pick up his stiletto, the guorella's corpse caught his eye, and the blood rushed to his head. He wanted to stomp on the already-dead guorella's head until it was no more than a bloody pulp. He wanted to kill it. Kill it dead.

It was already dead. This one, that is. This male guorella. But there were others.

Yeah. I still have more to kill, don't I? Kill them.

I'll kill them.

I should kill them. That's right. I'll wipe them all out.

Yeah. That's it.

That was exactly what I should be doing, isn't it? Kill them. Kill them. Kill them. Kill them. Kill them. Kill them. Kill them. Kill them. Kill. Kill. Kill. Kill. Kill. Kill, kill, kill, kill, kill, kill, kill, kill, kill, kill, kill, kill, kill.

You can't.

He heard a voice.

It was her voice.

When he saw the guorella's dead body, she came into his vision, too. He tried not to see.

No, that wasn't it. He should have been able to see, but he tried to convince himself he couldn't.

Even though she was right there.

He didn't want to see.

"...That's right, huh?"

Snapping and plunging in desperately...that wasn't his style. If he had above average strength, or some sort of special ability, it might be valid to throw safety to the wind and take a gamble, but unfortunately Haruhiro was a plain and mediocre person. Even if there wasn't a lot he could do, he had to do it to the best of his ability. Like always. Using his tools to their utmost, he'd find a way to survive. If he lost himself, he'd only self-destruct.

That might be fine, though.

If he self-destructed.

It didn't matter what happened. What did he care?

No.

Didn't she just tell him that he couldn't? Yeah. There was no way that was okay. But why had he heard her voice?

There was no way he should have.

He couldn't have—

Why...? That's right, her voice... Was I imagining it? It was an illusion... No, I mean, I definitely heard it—but there's no way... No—this is no good. Don't think. It's no good—I can't think about it. Pick it up. Pick the stiletto up. Then do what I have to—do the things I have to do. Do them.

He gritted his teeth. He braced both his legs. They were full of strength. He could do this.

The jail. This was the jail where Setora was being held. The guorellas were outside. They'd rushed the jail, and Yume and Kuzaku were barely holding the guorellas off as they tried to swarm in.

"Shihoru, use magic!" he shouted and tried to take off running.

But his knee gave out, and his hips sank. He clicked his tongue.

What was this? What the hell was this?

His body wouldn't move the way he wanted it to. Why? That was beyond obvious. He was spent. He'd killed guorella after guorella and, though he hadn't meant to, he'd gotten carried away. He'd lost too much blood, and he must have exceeded his stamina at some point, too. This was the result.

This... No... Forget about it. I have to forget.

Running in an incredibly awkward and unbalanced way, he rushed to the entrance. Setora, who was standing in the doorway, looked back to him.

"Haru!" She called his name, and their eyes met. Without responding, he went out.

Kuzaku was about two meters from the jail, letting out short battle cries as he swung his large katana around and went on a rampage. He probably was caught up in it and not thinking.

Kuzaku was being supported by his power of will. If he stopped, he'd surely collapse.

Yume moved quickly, her posture low, keeping any guorella that came close in check. Obviously, she had no extra strength to spare, but she didn't look like she was desperate. That was Yume for you.

Unfaltering and without fear, she constantly changed her positions left and right, occasionally passing behind Kuzaku, and supported him as best as she could. But it was a lot of moving. Yume couldn't last like that.

"Yume! I'll take the left side!" Haruhiro called.

"Meow!"

"I can still keep going!" he added.

Honestly, he didn't know if he could or not. Even so, he had to assume he could. To believe in it, and make his comrades believe, too.

Haruhiro drew his knife with the hand guard using his left hand. He moved up to Kuzaku's left, used Swat on the right arm of a guorella that happened to be leaping at him at the time, and then stabbed it in the face with his stiletto. When he immediately went for the eyes with his knife, it backed off.

On to the next one. It would be coming soon. Or rather, it was already here.

Haruhiro spun around to avoid an onrushing guorella.

Kuzaku cried, "Urgh!" and hit it with his large katana.

Its dark brown shell-skin shattered like a hard exoskeleton, and fragments flew everywhere. What destructive power.

The guorella backed away, unable to take it, and another guorella charged in. It was a young male, but if Haruhiro took it head-on, he'd be at a disadvantage. Even so, there was no room for retreat.

And so, rather than retreat, rather than stand his ground, he moved in. Taking the risk to close the distance, he decided to land a stiletto-and-knife combo on its face before it could hit him.

Unlike Kuzaku, Haruhiro lacked the power to break their shell-like skin, so while that wouldn't be much damage, it would be enough to crack it.

When that one retreated, the next, and then the next, and then the next...the guorellas kept pushing in, but they didn't attack in unison.

Even with humans, it was harder than it seemed to gang up on a single person and beat on them as a group. One guy had to grab the enemy from behind, another had to punch him in the face, another in the stomach, and if they couldn't divide the work like that, it wouldn't go well. Even if it was just two people whaling on one, their ally would get in the way more than it might be expected. In that case, the thing to do was make the enemy trip, or hold them down, and prevent them from moving. Naturally, their target—which was to say Haruhiro—was more than aware of that, so he didn't stay put.

Move.

He couldn't move as swiftly as usual.

I don't care. Move.

He kept moving and struck the enemies that came out. He just kept on repeating that. For as long as he could. Until his strength ran out.

Do it. Keep doing it. Soon enough, Shihoru will support us with magic. Even Setora will try to do something. Believe in my comrades, and do what I can. Get through this. That's all I can do. Now.

Grimgar of Fantasy and Ash

2 | Why Was I Born?

QUIETLY.

First and foremost, quietly.

Don't let my footsteps make noise.

Inch forward.

Ranta wasn't a thief or a hunter, but his creeping had to be top class by now. Was this a case of Big Daddy being the father of development?

What? That wasn't how the saying went? Was it "Necessity is the godmother of invention"? Well, whatever, it was a skill he desperately needed, so of course he was going to improve as he did it.

Good, good.

Just a bit further.

It's in the grass.

Its slimy skin was spotted green and brown. Its rear legs were bent, and its front legs were lifting up its body. Its round eyes weren't looking his way.

It's okay, Ranta told himself. *It's not moving. That means it hasn't noticed me yet.*

Still...it's huge.

No matter how you cut it, that thing looked like a frog. He'd have given eight-to-nine out of ten odds that it was definitely a frog, but it was a fist-sized—no, a baby-sized frog.

It's a big one, he thought. *Yeah. No matter what, isn't that too big...?*

Suddenly, a doubt crossed his mind. *Is it really a frog?*

Could there even be such a large frog? He was no expert on frogs, but it wouldn't be that strange if there was. That was the feeling he got. Even with dogs, there were small breeds and large breeds. With such a froggy silhouette, it had to be a frog. It was just huge, that was all.

But what about poison?

Poison, huh...? He hadn't been thinking about that at all.

He didn't remember clearly, but weren't there poisonous frogs, too? Well, most living beings that were poisonous looked poisonous.

Right? Maybe not, huh? Like with snakes, poisonous or not, they didn't look all that different, did they? Mushrooms, too. The mushrooms that looked poisonous could be surprisingly edible, and the ones that looked like you could totally eat them were sometimes bad news, too. Not that mushrooms were animals. Still, they were living beings all the same.

No, no, no! he told himself. *Don't waver. Yeah, this is no time to be indecisive. I'm hungry here.*

If he didn't eat it, he'd die. Well, maybe not, but he knew it would be best to eat something now while he still had the strength to do so.

Once he could no longer move properly, even securing food to eat would become difficult. He could move around now, but he wasn't an expert on surviving in the wild like a hunter, so it wasn't that easy to find edible things.

Birds and beasts were stupidly cautious, and when he tried to get close, they ran away. He could probably get bugs somehow, but if possible, he wanted to avoid eating them, so he'd be keeping that as a last resort.

So what about frogs? When he thought about it, he didn't have any misgivings. In fact, they seemed like they might be a real feast.

If he just jumped on the frog that was about a meter in front of him and bit into it whole, that'd be gross, but if he skinned it first, couldn't he make it tasty?

His mouth started to water.

All right, he told himself.

If it was poisonous, he'd cross that bridge when he came to it. If his tongue tingled, he could just spit it out. He had confidence in his danger sense and his reflexes.

I'm gonna eat, he decided. *I'll catch it and eat it. I'll eat it good.*

He came close to shouting his skill name out of force of habit, but he forced himself not to.

Here I go. Without a word! Silent Leap Out!

He leapt straight forward and reached out with both hands. That was exactly when it happened.

It jumped, too.

"Wha...?!"

His left and right hand grasped nothing as they collided with one another. How could this be? Had he let it get away?!

Its quick reaction to perceived danger and incredible jumping ability shocked him. With one leap, it had moved a full two meters. It was no ordinary frog, after all.

"Dammit! You're not getting away!" he shouted.

If that's how this is going to be, I'll get serious. Yeah. Without realizing it, I was underestimating it. Huge though it might be, I thought it was just a frog. Don't think of that thing as a frog. Think of it as an enemy to be struck down.

"Ungh! You're dead! Leap Out!" He jumped.

"Leap Out!" He jumped.

"Leap Out!"

"Leap Out!"

"Leap Out!"

He jumped, not giving it—or himself, for that matter—time to breathe. "Leap Out, Leap Out, Leap Out!"

He jumped, and jumped, and jumped after it. Each time he closed in with Leap Out, he reached out to capture it. However, each and every time, it dodged him at the last possible second. It wasn't even looking at him. It always had its butt turned his way. It was like it had eyes on its back.

The moment he thought that, he realized that on its back, what had looked like spots near its butt were actually eyelids.

No doubt about it. Those were eyelids. It had eyes on its back, or more like on its butt, too.

"Gross!" he shrieked. "Leap Out is what I'll feint with, and then...?! Then...?!"

When he went to jump and then didn't, the frog also started to jump and then stopped.

"Heh! Got you!"

He threw off its timing, then used Leap Out. This would clinch it.

It would—or it was supposed to, but the frog still slipped through his fingers and got away.

"Just how good are you?!" he raged.

This isn't just any enemy, he fumed. *What a powerful enemy it is. I have to see it as my fated rival now. I won't let it get away. I swear I'm going to take it down. I'll eat it, no matter what. How could I live without eating? I'm so hungry that my stomach's pressed damn flat. What does that even mean? I don't know, you damn frog! Damn you, frog! You're just a frog! A damn frog!*

Thus he leapt tens...no, hundreds of times. Seriously.

Man, he was tired. Seriously, seriously. Of course he was tired.

"But thanks to that, man," he muttered... "Bah!"

He tried to let out a big laugh, but only a small one came out.

In the hot, humid forest, he was all alone, sweaty, standing there with a much-too-large frog clasped in his hands. What was one to make of this situation?

"Damn, I'm cool..." he muttered.

Huh?

Was that it?

It was hard to say, but whatever the case, he'd reached his objective. The big frog that had been flailing all of its legs until a moment ago had finally given up and was being quiet now. However, having eyes on its butt was creepy, to say the least. They were blinking, too. Staring at him.

"D-don't look," he said. "I'm gonna eat you now..."

The big frog croaked. Was it begging for its life? That was futile, of course. In the end, this world was built on survival of the fittest, and the food chain. He couldn't fight on an empty stomach.

"Don't hold this against me... Nah, I guess it's okay if you do. If you want to resent me, resent me. I'm A-Okay with that. It's not like I'm trying to act tough or anything."

With that smooth line, he used his spare knife to quickly end the frog's life, skin it, pluck out its eyeballs, remove the internal organs, and—what was he to make of this? It was shaped like a frog, albeit a big one, but inside it, there was a lump of delicious-looking light pink meat. He wished he could cook it, but it'd be bad to start a fire. He had no water to wash it with, either.

Looks like I just have to chow down like this, huh? Here goes. Don't be afraid. There's nothing to be scared of. The world is all one?! No spice is better than hunger! I'm gonna eat. Eat. Eat it. Eat!

Theeeeeeere! How's that?!

He ate it. Ate it good. He spit out the bones, but the rest he completely devoured.

"Honestly, yeah," he muttered.

Throwing both his hands down on the ground, he squinted in the faint light that streamed through the leaves.

"The taste... Yeah. It wasn't good, or anything like that. It felt more like, 'Well, I ate something, at least.' That's important, huh? Yeah. It didn't make my tongue tingle, and my belly doesn't hurt. For now, that is. I'll bet I can move for days on this. It probably—"

He burped, and it made him scowl despite himself. It had a froggy, raw stench to it.

"...It's proof I'm still alive."

Yeah.

I'm alive. I want to shout it out loud.

I'm alive!

I'm living like crazy!

How do you like that?!

My life rocks!

He wasn't gonna shout it, though.

"Ranta!" a voice shouted.

Hearing his name called, Ranta nearly jumped up—but no, he absolutely couldn't do that. In times like this, rather than scramble around in a panic, it was better for him to be prepared to move right away if he needed to.

He wouldn't stand up. He'd stay a little more than half crouched, his upper body leaning forward.

Where had that voice come from?

Not nearby. From the way it sounded, the speaker was tens of meters away, maybe about a hundred meters.

He'd been lurking around Thousand Valley for over ten days now. He had no clue where he currently was. He'd gotten out of the thick fog, at least. This area had morning mist, but that was all, and right now there was hardly any haze at all. However, the thick trees and uneven topography made visibility bad.

"Ranta! I know you're there, Ranta!"

There was that voice again. Was it closer than last time? Well? He couldn't say for certain.

"Damn that old man," Ranta muttered, covering his mouth with the palm of his hand.

I know you're there, Takasagi had said.

Really? That wasn't a bluff? Unlike the frog he'd just eaten, this was a shrewd old man. His intuition was sharp, so he might have a vague idea of roughly where Ranta might be, but he probably hadn't pinned down his exact location.

If he knew exactly, there would be no need to shout out and alert Ranta. He'd just have to creep in. If he wasn't doing that, it meant Takasagi hadn't found Ranta yet.

Also, it was guaranteed that Onsa wasn't working with him. That goblin beast master had tamed black wolves and nyaas. Onsa's nyaas had been devastated, and there were only a few left, but the pack of black wolves led by his big black wolf Garo was intact. If Onsa were around, the black wolves would have already sniffed Ranta out and be closing in.

This was just Takasagi and some orcs or undead. He could get away. Or, at the very least, he still thought he had some chance to slip away.

He had to act calmly. That was the main thing.

They were waiting for him to panic and come out. So he wouldn't move. He was just going to stay put for now. Then he'd watch the area around him.

Open his eyes wide. Perk up his ears.

About three meters in front of him, there was a tree that was awfully twisted, to the point that it looked like a mass of tangled tentacles. Ranta walked next to that tree, keeping his footsteps silent. Was it a single tree? Or was it a mass of many different trees? Well, what did it matter?

Ranta leaned against that tree. Quietly, he took a deep breath.

"Ranta!" Takasagi shouted. "Come out, Ranta! Do it now, and I won't kill you, Ranta!"

This time, it was a little closer—maybe?

Takasagi was probably closing in little by little. But he wasn't super close yet.

Do it now, and I won't kill you, Takasagi had said.

Was he going to forgive Ranta for joining Forgan and then escaping? If Takasagi forgave him, Jumbo probably wouldn't say anything. He might even accept him as a comrade again.

No, no, Ranta told himself. *Takasagi only said he wouldn't kill me. Even if he doesn't take my life, he's still gotta plan on doing something terrible to me, right? There's no way he's going to laugh it off and let it slide. Well, of course not, right? I mean, I betrayed him, after all.*

"Ranta...!"

How many times had that voice yelled at him? He thought back...

"I'll use this scrap of wood," the old man said. Then he picked up not just any scrap of wood, but a thin, dry, twisted old branch, before gesturing to Ranta with his chin. "You use your own sword, Ranta."

"That's a pretty big handicap, old man... Don't underestimate me!"

It made him angry, but Ranta drew RIPer like he was told to and prepared himself.

He had gotten his hands on this weapon at Well Village in Darunggar, or rather he'd bought it from the blacksmith. It was a two-handed sword, but the blade wasn't that long, and it was lighter and easier to use than it looked. The ricasso at the base of the blade had a protuberance, and he was fond of its vicious appearance. It would be no exaggeration to say that Ranta had cut down many enemies with this beloved sword of his.

You think you can take it on with that branch? Don't be full of yourself, old man— was not a thing he thought, though.

Takasagi lowered his left hand—which he was holding the branch with—slightly, and stood up straight with his knees unbent.

He was about two meters away from Ranta.

If Ranta stepped into it, a slash or thrust would hit. What was more, Ranta was a dread knight, someone who specialized in high speed movement. He could reduce that distance to nothing in an instant.

Takasagi didn't even have his arm up, and all he had was a branch anyway. Even if he hit Ranta, it wouldn't hurt at all. It shouldn't have been scary at all.

Yet his breathing had grown strained. His feet...no, his whole body was cowering.

The old man could kill me at any time.

No, that couldn't be right. It was a branch, you know? A branch. That, and a look on the guy's face. His single eye was half open, his neck slightly tilted, and his jaw slack.

It was an expression that made Ranta want to complain. *I humiliated myself asking you to train me, and you agreed, even if it was only reluctantly. Come on, man, take this seriously. Shape up.*

Had this man just woken up? Was he hung-over or something? Despite that, why...?

Ranta couldn't win.

No matter how he had attacked, he couldn't win.

Did it only feel that way? Takasagi could see through Ranta completely. Was that overrating him?

Ranta could test it. If he did, he'd know for sure.

"What's wrong?" Takasagi lifted up the branch, finally, but then all he did was move his wrist and twirl it around. "Come at me, Ranta. You want to get strong, right? If you stay there cowering, you're never gonna make any progress."

"...Yeah, I know that." Ranta's voice quivered slightly when he responded.

"Do you really understand?" Takasagi wore a slight smile. "That's doubtful."

Now's the time!

It wasn't something he decided. You could say it was his wild instincts. Ranta's body sensed something and reacted.

It had felt perfect. Leap Out followed by Hatred. Basically, he'd jumped in and slashed downwards. It was simple, but a one-hit kill. He didn't hold back at all.

If Takasagi had been holding a sword, he might barely have been able to block it. But not with a branch. He couldn't hope to avoid it, either. This one strike was unavoidable. Ranta could say with confidence that it was a perfect Hatred.

Takasagi took a step to the left, and simply let RIPer go by. He stroked RIPer slightly with his branch, then struck Ranta in the face with it.

"Wha?!"

Did he see it coming?!

"It's written on your face." Takasagi planted a kick on the back of Ranta's knee to throw him off balance, then pushed him in the back with his foot.

Ranta pitched forward. "Whoa!"

"You're weak."

"Urgh!" Ranta rolled forward. "Dammit!" He instantly turned around, only to be hit in the face with that branch again. "Ack!"

"This is easy," Takasagi said.

Ranta had taken a whole lot of punches and kicks before falling over, and when he tried to get up again, he was punched and kicked. RIPer was no longer in his hands. He'd dropped it at some point. He couldn't lay a hand on Takasagi.

He flipped over, hitting his back and rear end, and as he lay flat on his back writhing, Takasagi sat down on his stomach.

"Gwuh!" Ranta yelped.

"You don't have it together at all. What do you mean, you want to get stronger? Don't make me laugh, you pissant."

"You said yourself...that you weren't always strong...didn't you...?"

"Well, yeah," Takasagi said, sneering. "But, thinking about it, I don't think I was as bad as you."

"If it were the you of ten years ago...you said...even I could've beaten you..."

"Don't take that nonsense seriously, you moron. Even the me of ten years ago was obviously a hundred times stronger than the you of right now."

"Th-that's...harsh..."

"You make a lot of extraneous moves." Takasagi tossed the branch, put his pipe in his mouth, and started smoking.

There he goes, puffing away while sitting on someone else's stomach. Who does he think he is, dammit? If I tried to throw him off, it's not like I couldn't. But I bet I'd take another pounding right away. What should I do...?

"There's something losing an eye and an arm taught me," Takasagi told him. "Humans—well, I guess this goes for orcs and other races, too, but we end up carrying all these things we don't need without realizing it. Getting stronger isn't about increasing the number of moves you make. It's about trimming the fat, and polishing what you have. It's about how much you can do what you need to do, without doing anything unnecessary. Ranta, you don't seem like you'd be good at that."

"Don't say that...like every part of me...is unnecessary..."

"After losing my arm..." Takasagi blew smoke, and wound back his left arm. Then he silently swung it down.

Oh, crap!

Takasagi had only swung his left arm. However, the katana in his left hand, its arc... Ranta could imagine it vividly. It didn't exist, but Ranta could see it.

"I did nothing but swing my katana," Takasagi said. "I was right-handed, after all. I realized that if I was going to live with just my left arm, I was going to have to break it in. Every day, every single day, I swung and swung and swung until I collapsed."

"Work hard, you're saying?" Ranta asked.

"Hard work is worthless."

"No, but you were just saying..."

"Why did I keep swinging my katana so much? Simple. In the beginning, I couldn't do it as well as with my right hand, and that pissed me off. But, you know, at some point, it started getting interesting."

"...Seriously?"

"Seeing what was wrong, how I could do better, and such. Noticing things, fixing them, testing things out. That repetition was interesting."

"That's one warped fetish," Ranta muttered.

"Do you think that without thinking, just continuing to swing, I could get my left arm as good at using a katana as my right had been? Sure, even if that was the only thing I did, like an idiot, I'd get some degree of growth out of doing it. Only to a certain degree, though."

"You're saying I'm not thinking?" Ranta accused him.

"Not enough, that's for sure. Normal people have to use their bodies until they collapse, and then they can finally see the difference between them and a genius."

"Even I know that," Ranta muttered.

"You must know a really strong guy or two," Takasagi said. "But the way you are now, all you know is that they're awesome. How exactly are they different from you? What could you do to trip them up? You have no idea, right?"

"I've got an idea, at least..."

"I've thought up a thousand ways to beat our boss, and three of them I'm confident would work."

"Beat Jumbo?" Ranta asked, dumbfounded.

"The boss knows this, but my goal is to kill him."

Ranta couldn't believe it. "Why would you want to kill Jumbo?"

"The boss's the one who lopped my arm off, you see. I don't hold it against him, but if I can, I want to kill him before I die. If I could kill the boss, that'd have to feel pretty great. I'd be happy, with no regrets left. It'd be amazing, and—I'm sure all that'd be left after that is to die."

"You really are crazy."

"You think?" Takasagi asked. "It's my life's goal. Having one gives me something to strive for."

"...Life's goal..."

Do I have one of those? Ranta wondered.

When he asked himself that...faces came to mind.

Not one. Several faces.

No way, he thought. *Why their faces? That's crazy. They're my life's goal? What the hell? It makes no sense.*

I only met them by chance, and was only working with them for a brief time in the long, long life ahead of me. Sure, in Darunggar, I thought at times I might be with them until the day I died. But that was simply because the situation made it appropriate to think so. There were some friendly folks in Darunggar, so I might have found myself a partner like Unjo did, and I might have broken up with them. Who would hang out with those guys forever by choice? Moguzo was different. He was my partner, but the others, they were only comrades.

You could say we only knew each other through work. With them, I never felt at ease, or that they were where I belonged, honestly. We had a basic level of trust, but I didn't like them, and they didn't like me. It was less mutual recognition, and more that we compromised and put up with one another.

This place isn't like that. Forgan's different.

Only a few of them understood the human language, and they didn't get clingy, and he was mostly left to his own devices, but it was strange how rarely he felt ostracized. Naturally, there had to be some of them who were less than fond of Ranta. He wasn't trusted. Despite that, he was being accepted.

What was he to make of this? He couldn't be trusted, and there was no way they did trust him, but they treated him like an ordinary comrade. Maybe this openness, this ease, was what was creating this unique sense that it felt good to be here.

Probably it was all up to how he acted from here. He just had to act in a way that said, *I'm definitely one of you guys.* If he did that, everyone would gradually grow to trust him. He'd eventually join their circle of friends. It was a shame there were no women, but that also meant he didn't have to be considerate of any women's feelings, so there were ups and downs to it.

He closed his eyes.

He could easily imagine a future here.

He'd fit in more and more, living every day with good humor. Even if he rebelled occasionally, there were people who'd take him down a peg and make him apologize. He'd have chances to go as wild as he wanted, too.

That outfit Jumbo wore, he liked it. It was cool. If he got his hands on that, he'd wear it over his armor.

Nah, maybe he wouldn't even need armor. Jumbo didn't wear any, after all. Yeah. Mobility was his greatest asset, so he was better off without heavy armor, honestly.

No matter what the attack, if it didn't land, he was fine. He just had to dodge, right? He could learn to dodge. What would he need to do to get to that point? There were people here he could ask about that.

What he had always wanted... He couldn't quite put into words what it was, but whatever it was, he felt like it was here.

"Ranta!" Takasagi called his name.

"...Yeah?"

No matter how he looked, it had never seemed like he'd be able to have it. That's why he'd half...no, mostly given up on it.

There was no place he'd fit in, and no one could ever understand him. Why did he feel that way? He didn't know. Was there some trigger, and after that, he'd started to think it? Even if there had been a trigger, it must have been before coming to Grimgar. He couldn't remember it.

It doesn't feel right, he thought. *Nothing ever does. No matter where I am. My heart's on edge. Or it was, huh? Now, maybe not so much.*

"What?" Ranta asked.

"Do you really want to become strong?"

Was that his life's goal? That was what Takasagi was asking.

For instance, if he wanted to get stronger, was that the goal? Or was getting stronger only a means to an end, and did he want to accomplish something with that strength? Or was the desire to get stronger an escape, and was he just averting his eyes from what he needed to face?

What do I want to do? What's my wish? he wondered. *I have no idea. Like I ever would.*

"Get off me already, old man," he muttered. "How long are you going to sit on my stomach? I'm not a chair, okay?"

"Not gonna happen." Takasagi laughed a low laugh. He put leaves in his pipe and lit it with what looked like a lighter. It took skill to do that with one arm. "Whatever the case, if you want to get stronger, I don't mind training you, but—"

"Please do." Ranta was surprised to find he said those words easily, and without hesitation.

Takasagi seemed a little surprised, too, but after a short silence, he said, "Well, fine then."

It was a response that maybe made sense, or maybe didn't.

3 | Jesus Again

"**I** CAN KEEP GOING." Kuzaku had been mumbling that to himself for a while now. "I can keep going. I can. I can keep going. I still can."

While muttering that to himself, he rammed his large katana into a guorella's mouth. When the tip of his sword burst out of the back of its head, Kuzaku pushed the creature back. He pushed, which pushed it over. Then, rather than pull his large katana free, he turned his wrist over and slid it to the side.

The large katana exited the guorella through its right cheek, and while Kuzaku muttered, "I can keep going," he stomped on the fallen guorella, and took a slash at another one that was nearby.

"I can keep going. I can. I can keep going. I can keep going, I can still keep going."

He'd been panting for a good while now. Kuzaku wasn't moving quickly at all. In fact, he even seemed to be going slowly.

Urgh... His head leaned back, and he wound up for a swing of his large katana.

Ungh...! He swung down.

It couldn't have been a bigger swing. How could a slash like that connect? How could it so easily break through the shell-like skin that covered the guorellas' entire bodies?

He was wheezing painfully, and there was no doubt he was in agony, but between those labored, far too labored breaths, he whispered, "I can keep going. I can. I still can. I can. I can keep going. I can. Still..."

He didn't stop. His large katana seemed to move with a will of its own, seeking enemies, and it was as if Kuzaku was being pulled along by it.

Because he was thoroughly exhausted, he couldn't restrain himself or dig in, and rather than Kuzaku swinging the large katana, the large katana seemed to be swinging him around.

No, that wasn't true. That wasn't it.

Most of the time, paladins remained cautious when they swung. Basically, they didn't swing with their whole body, only their arms.

If they stepped in as far as they could, swinging their body with the attack, that increased the attack's power, but it would inevitably create openings and neglect their defense. That was why paladins protected themselves with their shields, and worked to cover their comrades while attacking with quick slashes and thrusts. If the perfect chance didn't come along, they wouldn't unleash a full-force blow. That was the solid fighting style of the paladin.

That wasn't Kuzaku now.

Not only was he swinging with his arms, but he was also throwing his whole body into it as he swung through with his large katana. What was more, each swing, without exception, was desperate, throwing safety to the winds.

"I can still...guh—keep going...!"

Kuzaku slashed another guorella diagonally. Honestly, it was a surprise. Kuzaku's large katana cut a straight line from its left shoulder to its right hip, severing it in two.

That guorella had faltered and tried to jump back right before it was hit. Kuzaku had caught it perfectly and cut it up.

"I can keep...going.... Gah! Still! I can... Hah! I can keep going...!"

While the guorellas weren't running around in pell-mell terror of Kuzaku, they were definitely hesitant to come out. Kuzaku was single-handedly dominating the guorellas.

But that wasn't going to last. There was no way it could.

"Oohrahh...!" Kuzaku bent backwards, swinging his large katana up with both hands.

Then he stopped.

He had to be well past his limits. He had fought beyond his limits, and reached a point he couldn't have reached otherwise. Now, his feet were slipping beneath him. There was nothing beyond that. Only a fall. If he fell, he wouldn't survive.

Haruhiro prepared himself for the day, not far off, when it would end up like this. How was his body? Honestly, he didn't know. Haruhiro worked up all his strength and ran.

How far could he go?

It wasn't just Kuzaku. Everyone—Haruhiro himself, Yume, Shihoru, and Setora (who was defending Shihoru with a head staff that wasn't hers)—they were all doing what they could. He tried to step forward, but he couldn't at first. His weapons were awfully heavy, and his field of vision strangely narrow. He wasn't thinking straight, either. It was the same for all of them, probably. They were using every ounce of power they had. They really were giving it their all.

Haruhiro suspected that anything he thought while in this state was going to be wrong. He believed he had a grasp of the situation, but maybe he didn't actually. Nothing was certain. Maybe there was actually nothing left he could do.

Even so, Haruhiro ran. He couldn't not.

The guorellas were trying to swarm Kuzaku. Haruhiro clung on to him. He'd made it, somehow. He pulled on Kuzaku as he shouted, "Shihoru!"

"Dark, cry out!"

Shihoru unleashed Dark the elemental. Dark let out an oscillating, otherworldly *shuvuvuvuvuvuvuvuvuvvuvuvuvu* sound as he flew.

While the guorellas were flinching, Haruhiro needed to get Kuzaku away from them. But where to? He didn't know. But even if he didn't, they had to go.

"Haru-kun!" Yume lent him a hand.

Oh...

"Haru!" Setora, too.

Even with the three of them, he was heavy. Kuzaku was a big guy, and unlike the others, he was wearing heavy armor. He had a helmet covering his head, too. To think he could fight like that with all this heavy equipment... It was nothing short of incredible.

Ultimately, Haruhiro, Yume, and Setora carried Kuzaku near the door to the jail.

"Spread out!" Shihoru called.

From the door, Shihoru swung her staff. The Dark that was flying around and intimidating the guorellas with his other-worldly noises burst, spreading in no time.

This was Dark in mist form. Dark Mist.

The guorellas heard a bizarre sound, and then they were blinded by black mist. That was more than they could take. Haruhiro couldn't see them through the black mist, but it looked like the guorellas were running around in confusion. If they could, he wanted them to stay that way.

Of course, that was asking for the impossible. Shihoru couldn't maintain Dark Mist forever. Or rather, she wouldn't last that long.

Kuzaku was sitting on the ground, his back against the jail wall. It might be more accurate to say that they'd sat him down there. If Haruhiro and the others didn't support him, Kuzaku would surely collapse. Yet still, Kuzaku was gripping his large katana as if it had become one with his arm, and made no attempt to let go of it.

"...I can keep going. Still...still... I can..." Kuzaku was

mumbling inside his helmet.

"I can still keep going." He was repeating those words that Haruhiro had said.

It's okay, you've done enough, Haruhiro wanted to say to him. But he couldn't.

If he said that, the very moment he did, Kuzaku would drift off somewhere, and he might never come back. It might break the string that was tying Kuzaku down to where Haruhiro and the others were.

Haruhiro was afraid. Afraid to call out to him. Afraid to leave him alone. Even at this very moment, Kuzaku might be about to leave them. If so, he had to call him back.

"Kuzakkun...!" In times like this, Yume's decisiveness helped.

When Yume called his name and shook his shoulder, Kuzaku took a short, shocked breath, and then tried to stand up in surprise.

Haruhiro was stunned. *You're kidding me. You can stand? I'm amazed you can even move!*

It looked like standing was beyond him, but Kuzaku lifted his visor with his left hand and glanced around the area.

"...Haruhiro. Everyone... Huh? Where's Merry-san?"

"Inside, resting."

Who was that? Haruhiro thought. Who had said that?

He soon realized, it was him. Though the words had come out reflexively, he was amazed he could be so deceitful.

Haruhiro was ashamed, but also thought, *This is fine.* The fact was, she was resting. It wasn't a lie, or so he tried to tell himself.

Or maybe that was just what he wanted to believe.

Yume looked into the prison from the door. Then, with a glance at the head staff Setora was carrying, she turned to face Haruhiro.

Haruhiro averted his eyes.

"I...see..." Kuzaku nodded repeatedly.

"Fooooooooooo, fooooooooooo, fooooooooooo!"

They heard a voice from inside the black mist. It was pretty close, too. No, not pretty close, really close.

Was it coming?

That one?

When a male guorella matured, the hairy horns that densely covered the area from the back of its head to its back like a mane turned red. A guorella troop was usually centered around one of these powerful redbacks, with a number of females that were its mates, along with their offspring. However, the troop that had pursued Haruhiro's party all this way, and was now attacking Jessie Land, was different. It had multiple redbacks, and an awfully large number of members.

Was it an especially large and powerful redback leading multiple troops? That had been Haruhiro's hypothesis. There had, in fact, been an exceptionally large redback in this troop, but Kuzaku had taken it down.

Even with that oversized redback dead, the guorellas had not been disturbed by it, and were still rampaging around. That large guorella hadn't been the leader of this exceptional troop.

Probably, it was this one.

One of the redbacks pressed through the veil of black mist

and appeared. It was no coincidence that its eyes met Haruhiro's. It was looking at Haruhiro with intent. Like it had been searching for him, and had found him.

The shell-like skin covering its face wrinkled up. Had it smiled? Another smile.

There was no doubt about it. It was the smiling redback. That one was the leader of this troop.

Haruhiro tried to call out and warn the others.

"Every—whuh..."

The redback turned heel. It faded into the black mist, and he could no longer see it. Haruhiro was dumbstruck. What had that been just now?

"Foooooooo, foooooooooooo, fooooooooooooooo!"

He heard that voice in the black mist again.

"Ho!"

"Heh!"

"Hoh! Hoh!"

"Heh, heh, heh!"

"Ho! Ho! Ho! Ho!"

The guorellas began shouting, and it echoed.

Oh. So that was how it was.

While feeling shame at how dull he'd been, Haruhiro realized... It had come to confirm their location for itself. Then, rather than take them out itself, it was having its fellow guorellas do the job.

So? he wondered. *What now?*

There isn't a moment to lose. I have to do something. Anything. Is there anything I could do?

I don't see what.

"Nobody die!" Haruhiro shouted.

Those words weren't an order. They weren't even encouragement. They were simply Haruhiro's wish. One with little chance of coming true, at that.

"Scatter!" Shihoru swung her staff. The black mist that was spread out dispersed. Shihoru didn't miss a beat before summoning Dark again. "If we kill that redback...!"

"...'Kay!" Kuzaku tried to get up using his large katana for support.

Just when it looked like he couldn't get up, Yume gave him a hand. "Mew!"

"Very impressive..." Setora said sarcastically as she readied the head staff.

At her feet was Kiichi, who had gotten there at some point, with his back arched and his hackles raised. It was like he was saying he was ready to fight along with his master.

The black mist had long since cleared, and Haruhiro could see the guorellas clearly. Two redbacks—no, three. More than ten young males. There were female guorellas behind them, and up on the roofs of the buildings, too. He didn't see the smiling redback.

I'm pretty calm, Haruhiro thought. He must have become defiant.

"Gahhhhhhhhhhhhhhhhhhhhhhhhhhhhh!" Kuzaku shouted, probably trying to psyche himself up, then moved forward.

His steps were heavy and slow. With both hands on the hilt, he was dragging his large katana behind him. Its tip cut a thin line in the ground.

Suddenly, the tip flew up.

His large katana drew a lightning-like trail.

The right arm of the redback right in front of him fell to the ground, along with its head.

Kuzaku nearly stumbled forward after that.

He dug in his feet just in time to stop himself, and his head bobbed down. Lowering his shoulders, he let out a deep breath. "Whew..."

There was a young male about to attack Kuzaku. Haruhiro grappled it from the front. Even though it was a young male and hadn't turned red yet, its mane of hairy horns was hard and sharp, and they stabbed into Haruhiro's body.

Like he cared. He pounded his stiletto through the young male's left eye. The young male twitched. Haruhiro pulled on his stiletto, then thrust. He stabbed it in and out.

"Boooooooooooooooooooooooohhhhhhhhh!" the young male howled.

It tried to grasp Haruhiro's head with its right hand. It grabbed Haruhiro's left flank with its left hand, trying to pry Haruhiro off of itself.

All he could do was twist the stiletto. Stab, and stab, and try to strike a fatal blow.

Die, die, die. Come on, please, die.

The young male's hand—no, its entire body—went limp.

It collapsed to the ground. Before that, Haruhiro got away from it. But he didn't have time to catch his breath.

"Haru!" Setora cried.

Behind him and to the left. There was another guorella about to pounce on Haruhiro. A redback, what's more.

"Go!" Shihoru shouted.

If Shihoru hadn't sent out Dark in the nick of time, Haruhiro might have been pushed down by that redback, and snuffed in an instant.

Dark sunk into the redback's left shoulder. The redback shuddered. Blood flowed out of its eyes and nose. The redback was stumbling. However, it wasn't dead yet, so it might still recover.

Haruhiro rushed over to the redback, thrusting his stiletto into its right eye up to the hilt.

Not yet. One strike wasn't enough. He needed to kill it good and dead. He fully intended to do that.

"Gahhhh!" Kuzaku went flying, and when Haruhiro looked over, it was there.

The smiling redback.

It hadn't been there before. It was back now?

It looked like Kuzaku had eaten a jumping kick from the smiling redback.

It turned towards Haruhiro. He thought it would smile, but it didn't. It slammed both its hands on the ground. Then, bending both its legs, it supported itself with its arms to swing its lower body like a pendulum, and—it came flying at him.

Haruhiro made a desperate jump to the side.

He rolled, then got up.

Had he avoided it? If he hadn't, he'd probably be dead about now.

What about the smiling redback? Where was it? He couldn't afford to be looking for it.

A young guorella barreled towards him while shouting something.

Haruhiro twisted to avoid it by a hair's breadth—oh, crap!

Haruhiro instantly leaned back, and a different guorella's violent swing went right past his nose. Then something grazed his right leg, and he fell. Reflexively, he let out a "Whoa!" despite himself, rolled desperately to get away from the guorella trying to stomp him, and hit something.

The wall of a building? The jail? Was he cornered? He had to fight back. To stand. To get up, then take it from there. He might not make it. Even if he didn't, though, he had to do it.

"Zahhhhh!" Kuzaku hollered.

Kuzaku.

Kuzaku, huh?

Is that Kuzaku?

Kuzaku slammed his large katana into the male guorella that was about to pound Haruhiro to death. "Ungh!" he cried. "Gahh! Take that! And that!" Again and again, he slashed. "Haru—" Until that guorella fell. "Hirohhhhhh!"

"Yeah!" Haruhiro jumped up.

What am I shouting "yeah" for? It's not over yet, he thought. *I'm not dead yet, so it can't end. Even if I lose someone, even if I'm sad, even if it hurts and it's painful—even then, if it was going to end, it would have already. But it can't end. The end doesn't come that easily. We can't let it end so easily.*

"Unghhhh!" Kuzaku swung his large katana. He probably aimed for a guorella, but he missed, and that guorella sent Kuzaku flying with a single blow.

The guorella got on top of the fallen Kuzaku.

"Argh!" Kuzaku desperately thrust out his large katana, and, through sheer luck, it pierced the guorella's chest.

However, it wasn't done yet. The guorella wasn't dead. The guorella raged.

"Gu, ho! Ga, ha!" It reached out for Kuzaku with both hands.

"Ungh! Gah!" Kuzaku tried to kick the guorella off him.

Haruhiro clung on to that guorella's back, stabbed his stiletto into its right eyeball, pulled it out, and stabbed, pulled it out, and stabbed. The guorella's body went limp.

When Haruhiro moved away, Kuzaku kicked the guorella's body away from himself. "Grahhhh!"

When Haruhiro tried to take Kuzaku's arm and pull him up, he felt something—he could only say that it was something, but when he looked seven to eight meters away, Yume was spread-eagled.

"Yume!"

Haruhiro let go of Kuzaku's arm. He tried to run in Yume's direction. A guorella ran in from the side and obstructed him.

Damn it. You're in my way. Don't get in my way. I've gotta get to Yume.

But Haruhiro didn't have the power to remove that guorella by force. Haruhiro's body wasn't responsive enough that he could slip past the guorella to get to Yume.

Dark flew in with a *vwooong,* and made a guorella start convulsing. However, it wasn't the guorella Haruhiro was facing. It was a different guorella that Kuzaku was trying to attack.

The guorella reached out for Haruhiro. He managed to dodge it at virtually the last possible moment. He was worried about Yume.

While managing to dodge the guorella's attacks somehow, he peeked at Yume.

Not a good idea. If he didn't focus on the enemy in front of him, it'd get him.

"Kuzaku, help Yume!" he screamed.

It was fine to try saying that, but what about Kuzaku? Was he in any condition to fight? The guorella kept coming at him, so he couldn't check.

He felt like he saw Yume jumping to her feet. However, he wasn't certain of it. That might have been because the enemy's offensive was tough, so Haruhiro was always a move behind.

If he lost his balance now, he'd likely get hit. If it landed even one shot, he couldn't take it. He couldn't even afford to be wasting time on this one. There were other enemies.

Lots of them. Too many.

"Delm, hel, en, giz, balk, zel, arve!"

Someone was chanting a spell. It wasn't Shihoru. The voice was different. Besides, Shihoru hadn't used any magic other than Dark in forever. But Haruhiro knew this spell. No, he'd probably heard a similar one.

Boom! An incredible shockwave, explosion, and heat came

straight at him, thrusting up from below, too.

Though Haruhiro wasn't sent flying, his head was knocked back, and he nearly collapsed. Haruhiro saw a number of guorellas pitched into the air.

It was an explosion.

There was a fairly wide scale explosion, and he understood in an instant that it had been the product of magic. He had some idea whose, too. If it wasn't Shihoru's, there was only one person left.

Jessie.

Haruhiro was almost…no, completely certain he was the one who'd done it.

"Damn it!" Haruhiro shouted as he stabbed his stiletto into the guorella rolling around on the ground and clutching its head next to him.

Damn it, if you could use this kind of magic, couldn't you have used it from the beginning? Shouldn't you have used it right away? Before the damage spread? If you'd done that…!

Haruhiro was shouting aloud as he finished off the panicking guorellas that had been sent flying by Blast, or perhaps a higher level version of the spell—although he wasn't sure if actual words were coming out, or if he was just shouting incoherently.

Here and there, he saw green-coated figures throwing bottles at the guorellas. They were the rangers, armed and trained by Jessie to defend Jessie Land. There were originally twenty-four of the rangers, but there had been casualties in the guorella attack. Even so, more than ten of them seemed to have survived.

The rangers weren't just hitting them with bottles. A number of the rangers had bows at the ready. What they had nocked to those bows weren't any ordinary arrows. The heads were on fire. They were fire arrows.

The fire arrows flew in. Without a longbow with a lot of power or a crossbow, it probably wasn't possible to pierce a guorella's shell-like skin. However, those fire arrows didn't need to.

Several guorellas were lit on fire. Most likely, those bottles were filled with a liquid. It looked like it was some sort of flammable oil or something. That liquid had been ignited by the flaming arrowheads.

It wasn't what you would call a blaze. But still, the guorellas were screaming and rolling around on fire. The flames spread from guorella to guorella, or to the ground where the liquid was splattered, and then spread.

Haruhiro lowered his posture, pulling up the collar of his cloak to cover his mouth. The smoke was incredible. The fire was starting to spread to the buildings, too.

The buildings of this village that was roughly in the middle of Jessie Land were mostly made of wood, and their roofs were thatch. Once the fire started, they'd burn down almost entirely before there was time to put it out.

It was hard to imagine the rangers had done this of their own volition. They were only following Jessie's orders. Jessie meant to burn the village, guorellas and all.

There might be villagers who were still trembling in their houses, having been unable to escape, but the vast majority had either been killed by the guorellas or had run away. If the buildings burned down, they could just build them again. If you thought about it that way, it wasn't a bad move—maybe?

Certainly, if there was any other way to exterminate this vicious and cunning guorella troop, Haruhiro couldn't think of it. Jessie might have been forced to make this hard decision because he had no other choice, but it was still hard to understand.

Jessie had advised Haruhiro to use the jail.

Haruhiro had understood why in an instant, and done as Jessie said. If they were surrounded by the guorellas in an open place, they wouldn't stand a chance. If they shut themselves up in as sturdy a building as possible, and defeated only the guorellas that came in, they could hold out for the time being.

However, as a result, Haruhiro had to say that it had been a serious, painful, and ultimately fatal mistake for them.

What was it to Jessie, then?

"...Bait. We were bait."

When Jessie had said, "Use the jail," he hadn't been offering advice. Most likely, he had intended to use Haruhiro and his group.

By setting them up as a decoy, drawing in the guorellas, and buying time that way, Jessie had used that time to set things up.

Haruhiro and the others had been bait dangled in front of the guorellas.

Didn't you sow the seeds of that yourself? he thought he heard a voice say, and it felt like the tears might start flowing.

Haruhiro and his group had brought the guorellas all the way here. Thanks to them, a great number of the residents of Jessie Land had died. If they were used as part of the effort to defeat the guorellas, that was to be expected. He was in no position to complain to Jessie about it. Did he think he had the right to criticize Jessie? There was no way he did.

But, oh... Still...

"Merry."

He called out her name. He hadn't wanted to. He didn't want to speak her name. Haruhiro was afraid.

He had the sense that once the thing that was vague and blurry for the moment became clear, it would take on an indisputable form, rise before him, and block his way. If possible, he wanted it to stay vague. Forever. Until the end of time, if possible.

If he could make it so it hadn't happened, he wanted to. If her absence remained vague and blurry, he could continue floating around with the hallucination that there might be some way to negate it. For instance, maybe this was all a dream. He'd wake up, and be relieved that, *Oh, it really was just a dream.* Somewhere in his heart he believed that was not completely impossible.

He'd probably see several of them after this. Dreams where she was still with them. In those dreams, *See, it was a mistake, she's here, why did I think I'd never see her again?* Haruhiro would think with a wry laugh. Then, he'd wake up. The worst possible awakening would come.

Haruhiro had already had that sort of experience, so he could very clearly imagine what his feelings would be like in that moment.

But still, Haruhiro tried to think. *If I can have dreams with her in them, it's not so strange that I'd have dreams where she's gone. So, since the sense that she's gone is so vague and blurry, this might actually be a dream. I mean, there's no way she could really be gone.*

It's a lie that Merry's dead.

He'd been used by Jessie, and Merry had died as a result.

Though, to begin with, if they hadn't led the guorellas here, this wouldn't be happening at all.

Haruhiro had made so many mistakes.

Because of that, Merry was dead.

She'd died right in front of Haruhiro's eyes.

She'd been killed.

No.

I practically killed her myself, didn't I?

At the very least, I let Merry die.

It was me.

It's my fault.

Sorry, Merry.

You smiled for me at the end, but why you smiled, I have no idea.

I mean, it was my fault, wasn't it? I let you die.

Even though you were my precious comrade.

Even though I liked you, Merry.

I loved you.

I couldn't protect Merry. Worse yet, if Merry hadn't intercepted the guorella coming into the cell that time, I might have been the one who died. It would totally have been me. Merry saved me.

It's thanks to Merry that I'm still alive.

I let Merry die, and here I have the gall to go on living.

"Haiiaaaaaaaaaaaaaaaaaaaaaaaaahhhhhhhh!" An incredible shout echoed.

It was immediately apparent who it was from.

The smiling redback.

It was less than ten meters from Haruhiro, howling at the sky. It wasn't smiling. Probably, it was enraged.

He could understand its feelings. Haruhiro felt the same, after all. This went beyond mere irritation or anger.

While there were many targets for its anger, most of the redback's rage was likely directed at itself. It—and Haruhiro, too—had been set up. More than the person who set them up, they found themselves unable to forgive themselves for falling for it.

"Weruu, ruu, ruuuu, ruu, ruu, weruuuuuuu!"

But this was no ordinary guorella. The smiling redback had been screaming into the empty sky a moment before. Then, suddenly, it jumped up and began making a strange call. That call, if Haruhiro recalled, was the sign to retreat.

Like I'd let you go!

Haruhiro ran. He couldn't run fast. The best he could do was a little more than a fast walk, but he still couldn't stop.

I know. I know you. Even if you back off now, you're sure to come back.

For as long as it lived, it would tenaciously pursue Haruhiro and his comrades. It was only making what might be called a strategic retreat so that it could continue that.

What can I do to end this?

"Weruu, ruu, ruuuu, ruu, ruu, weruuuuuuu!"

While calling out to its comrades, the redback was trying to run away.

It peeked in Haruhiro's direction.

It had noticed.

He still had another five meters to go before he reached it.

"Get that one!" Haruhiro shouted as he raced over.

Kuzaku, Jessie, the rangers, it didn't matter who. That thing. They had to do something about that thing. It needed to die here. They couldn't let it go. Or it would be in vain.

Her death, Merry's, would be in vain.

Having meaning or not wouldn't change it. That was the result, and the facts wouldn't change. But wasn't that just too sad? Shouldn't it at least have been for something?

Merry had died, and because of that Haruhiro had survived, and he was going to be able to take this redback down.

Never, in all eternity, was a story like that going to bring him any solace, and this wound would likely never heal. Because Merry, the one who healed his wounds, was dead. Nothing could fill this void. That was why, in the end, it was meaningless. No matter what Haruhiro did here, it was impossible to give Merry's death meaning.

Ugh, win or lose, I don't care anymore. For now, either I'm going to kill you, or you're going to kill me. One or the other.

He was going to end this.

It was time to settle things.

But it was fast.

Or was Haruhiro just slow?

Either way, the distance between them doubled in no time.

"Oorahhhhh!" One of the rangers threw a bottle at its face.

Cream-colored skin. Red eyes. It was that ranger. Yanni, or

whatever her name was.

The bottle shattered, the oil splattered everywhere, and the smiling redback was soaked. Paying the oil no heed, it continued racing away with its knuckle walk.

A different ranger loosed two or three fire arrows, but none found its mark.

"Delm, hel, en—"

He knew that was Jessie's voice, but where was that man? He couldn't see him. However, Jessie was chanting, and about to use magic. That was Arve Magic.

"Saras, trem, rig, arve!"

Where the smiling redback had been heading, a great column of fire that seemed like it could burn the sky rose up. The column of fire didn't weaken, and it stood in the smiling redback's way.

Firewall. Or its higher-level equivalent.

What was the smiling redback going to do?

It didn't stop.

It meant to dive straight in, even though it was soaked with oil. It meant to break through that column of fire without avoiding it and escape.

The column of fire was burning loudly with several nearby buildings having been caught in it. If it went straight through that fire, where would the redback come out?

Haruhiro estimated where it was heading, and took a route around the column of fire and burning buildings.

He found it.

Trailing flames, it was far ahead of him and racing away. It was almost out of the village.

Now it was out.

"Wait...!"

Even if he shouted that, it was never going to wait. Haruhiro ran. He nearly tripped and fell several times, but he pushed himself onward, and onward.

A damp, moist wind was blowing.

It was awfully dark.

Where were the other guorellas? About how many of them had escaped?

Like he cared.

It was none of his concern.

No—How was it not his concern? Besides, what was he chasing that one for, anyway? It was still running, but it was a ball of flame. That burning wasn't normal. Even if it was a guorella, it wouldn't come away from that unharmed. If he thought about it normally, it'd stop moving eventually. Probably, Jessie and his people would track it down and finish it. There was no need for Haruhiro to chase it.

Before that, weren't there other things he should be doing? What about his comrades, for instance? Were they okay? Shouldn't he turn back and verify that first? Why was he doing this?

He knew. He was doing something meaningless. Even if he knew that in his head, he couldn't stop. He didn't want to stop.

Haruhiro went outside the village, too. The sky was rumbling. Lightning.

The smiling redback was racing through the fields. The fields were thick with a wheat-like plant that was bearing grain. When the redback moved forward, it lit fire to that grain and scorched it. There was a trail clearer than footprints leading to where it was. Haruhiro just had to follow that. In the field, it was fine if he fell, because he could just get up again.

When he left the village, the smiling redback had been more than ten meters, maybe twenty, ahead of Haruhiro. How about now? Was it ten meters? No, closer. It was five, maybe six meters. Sometimes, he even felt like if he reached out, he could touch it. Its speed was definitely failing.

Haruhiro hadn't turned back once. He pursued the smiling redback without looking away.

Were Jessie and his comrades following behind him? Were there no other guorellas around? He didn't know. It wasn't that he wasn't concerned about that. He didn't want to know. It was no good that he was acting like this. No good at all.

But he wanted to end this.

He would catch that thing—which was still burning here and there, spreading smoke as it ran—and terminate it personally. With that, he wanted to end it all.

Merry. Merry would definitely be mad.

If it were Merry, she'd scold him. *Stop it,* she'd tell him. *Forget about me. You were with me up until now, and you were my comrade, and that was enough. Haru, keep moving forward like you were before.*

That seemed like the kind of thing Merry would have said.

You don't get it, Merry, he'd retort. *Nothing. You don't understand at all.*

I mean, you're super considerate of your comrades, you're a good person, and the best healer we could have, and—and, really, you're ridiculously pretty, and you've got a cute side, too, but somehow, Merry, there are times when you act like you're not good enough... even though that's not true at all. It could never be true.

I wanted to hold your hand tight.

It's presumptuous of me to say this, but I wanted to give you more confidence in yourself.

You were smiling more than you had in the past, but I wanted to make you smile more.

To tell you the truth, I wanted to hug you with all my might.

To take your hand, and keep walking together forever.

Merry.

Merry.

Merry.

I can't imagine a future without you.

Even in Darunggar, there was a sun that rose. But without you, Grimgar will be in total darkness. I won't be able to see anything. Or hear anything, either, I'm sure.

I can't move forward.

If that's the future that's waiting, I don't need it.

I mean, really.

I've had enough.

Let this be the last.

"Once I've killed you...!" Haruhiro worked up the last of his strength and pushed himself to go faster. That was when it happened.

The smiling redback fell forward.

Thanks to that, Haruhiro finally caught up to it.

It'd get up soon and recover, he was sure. It'd run, or it'd fight back. But who cared? Not him. It didn't matter.

It had fallen face down, with only its face turned to the side. Haruhiro jumped on its back. The flames on its body had been almost completely extinguished. It was just smoldering. It wasn't even that hot. But there was something strange.

It didn't even twitch.

"Hey..." Haruhiro murmured.

What was the meaning of this? Haruhiro mounted its back, and was in a position to stab his stiletto into its blatantly defenseless eyes at any moment. Despite that, he felt nothing.

Hey? Hey? Hey? Hey? What's wrong, huh? Are you biding your time, waiting for a chance to strike back? That's it, right? Say that's it, will you?

But still, it was weird. It was too different from before. Like it was a completely different thing now.

A different thing.

Yes, it was, indeed, a completely different kind of thing. There was no sign it was a living thing from it. It was just a thing now.

Haruhiro adjusted his grip on his stiletto.

There was no strength in his hand. Not just in his hand. In his entire body. Like there was a hole in it somewhere, and his vitality was flowing out through it. He had to find that hole quickly,

and plug it.

He knew what he had to do. That was decided, so all that was left was to do it. It was a simple thing. There was nothing hard about it. He could do it. There was no way he couldn't.

Now, do it, he told himself. *Do it. Hurry up.*

Scattered rain began to fall.

It was large drops.

It quickly picked up in intensity.

There was a crazy amount of thunder. The rain poured down like a waterfall.

Because of that, he didn't hear the footsteps. A man in a green coat came up to his side and said something to Haruhiro. Whatever he said to him, Haruhiro didn't get it. That was why he neither nodded nor shook his head.

That man with the blond hair and blue eyes—Jessie—knelt down, not so much next to Haruhiro as to the smiling redback. He peered at its face, taking a serious look. Particularly at its open eyes and its nose. Then Jessie grabbed its jaw and shook it around.

"Yeah... This thing's dead."

By that point, the rain had lessened a little. The thunder had stopped sounding, too. The sky was even beginning to brighten.

"The inside of its mouth is burned and swollen," Jessie said. "Judging from this, the burns probably reach its throat. It wasn't able to breathe properly. I'm impressed that it got this far. It must have run out of strength."

"...What the hell?" Haruhiro muttered.

Haruhiro rolled off its back and fell into the mud. The now lighter rain lashed at his cheeks.

What the hell was this?

Following after Jessie, a number of rangers gathered around.

"Haru-kun!" Yume cried.

"Haru!" Setora shouted.

"...Haruhiro-kun!" yelled Shihoru.

"Haruhiro!" Kuzaku called.

Hearing the voices calling his name, Haruhiro closed his eyes. He placed his left hand over his closed eyelids.

Haru-kun. Haru. Haruhiro-kun. Haruhiro.

There were voices for four people.

Four people.

"What happened to your priest?" Jessie asked.

Haruhiro couldn't answer immediately.

He moved his hand from over his eyes.

When he opened them, Jessie was looking down at him.

How was Haruhiro reflected in this man's unreadable blue eyes, which gave no indication of what he thought or felt?

It's your fault, Haruhiro almost said, but then, *That's wrong,* he thought and ground his back teeth. It might not actually be wrong, but he really felt it was.

"I see." Jessie blinked, then took a short breath. "So she died."

"...Don't say it."

"Hm?"

"Don't say it. Don't you...say that."

"I was only asking because you seem pretty badly hurt, and it looked like you could use some healing."

That doesn't matter. I don't care anymore. You get that. Don't you? Yeah, you probably don't.

You're weird anyway. You took a solid hit from my Backstab, but you seem just fine. You don't look like a mage, and you were apparently a hunter, but you can use magic. Incredible magic at that. You look human, but you're clearly not.

Haruhiro rolled over to lie on his front, then tried to get up. His comrades were coming. He couldn't lie around.

But his body felt heavy. So heavy. His arms and legs wouldn't push him up.

"Haru-kun!" Yume called.

In the end, Yume helped him up. Though he was up now, he couldn't stand without support. He wasn't just weak with exhaustion. Like Jessie had said, he noticed he was fairly seriously injured. He didn't feel much pain, but he was bleeding all over, and it looked pretty bad. If he didn't get treatment, he'd eventually pass out, and his heart would stop.

"Haru—Argh, you're in the way! Move, hunter!" Setora pushed Yume aside and held Haruhiro in her arms. "Are you okay? Hey, Haru, keep your senses. The guorella troop scattered. If this is their leader dead here, then we should be safe for the time being, at least. Listen, Haru, whatever else happened, we won."

"...We won?" he asked numbly.

"Yes. Even if you can't believe it, know that we won. For now—"

"We won..."

Haruhiro wanted to push Setora away. But even if he searched for the willpower to take on such a momentous task, he probably didn't have it left.

That was why Haruhiro just shook his head. Again and again.

Shihoru moved up next to the smiling redback's corpse. She wasn't just winded, she was almost completely out of breath. Shihoru sat down where she was.

Kuzaku tripped somewhere about six to seven meters behind Shihoru, and he didn't get up. Haruhiro could hear his wheezing, labored breaths all the way over here. That ranger that walked over to Kuzaku was probably Yanni.

"Yanni!" Jessie called out to her.

Yanni turned around and ran hurriedly back towards Jessie.

Jessie gave Yanni some sort of order. It was in a language Haruhiro couldn't understand, but the words "vooloo yakah" stuck in Haruhiro's ears. Maybe that was because when Yanni heard those words, a look of tension and fear came over her face.

When Yanni gathered the rangers and gave orders, he heard her use the words "vooloo yakah," too. The rangers led by Yanni split off into a number of groups and dispersed.

The rain had fully stopped, and the sun was even peeking through the clouds in places. It had apparently been a passing storm.

"Well, fortunately..." Jessie shrugged.

What was fortunate?! At that point, Haruhiro snapped.

Jessie said, "Our shaman survived, so assuming we heal the wounded immediately, the only problem is your priest. For now, we can't say anything until I see the state she's in, but—"

"Merry's...!" Haruhiro pushed Setora aside and closed in on Jessie. "She's dead! Merry died! I...I let her die! I don't want to hear this crap about the state she's in! What—What are you even talking about...?!"

"No, listen..."

Even with Haruhiro holding him by the collar, Jessie was unperturbed. He wasn't intimidated, but he didn't have a hint of a smile. It wasn't a blank look, either. Did this man even have emotions? Maybe he didn't have human emotions. This man's behavior was unnatural enough to make a person suspect that. Haruhiro thought so, and anyone who saw Jessie now would have had to agree.

"We can't say anything until I see the state she's in," Jessie said. "Did I not tell you that?"

"She died! There's no state to look at! We have to hurry... Hurry, before No-Life King's curse affects Merry... Before she ends up like her old comrades... Right, we can't let that happen to Merry..."

"The curse of Enad George, the No-Life King, huh?" Jessie snorted, and then scowled.

That was unnatural somehow, too. Maybe it was better to say it seemed disjointed.

"Enad George...?" Haruhiro repeated.

"Let go." Jessie hit Haruhiro in the chin. No, Jessie just pressed

his palm hard against Haruhiro's chin.

Despite that, Haruhiro flipped over.

Haruhiro struck his hip, and hit the back of his head. All the strength left his body.

Yume and Setora were protesting to Jessie. No matter what they said, Jessie didn't take them seriously.

Haruhiro moved just his eyeballs to look at the man. Jessie was creepily silent, and he was looking down at Haruhiro in a way that had no apparent implications.

"Her state..."

His voice was as weak as a mosquito's, and Haruhiro himself had no idea what he was trying to say.

No, the truth was, he knew. Haruhiro was trying to question Jessie. But it was ridiculous. After all, Merry had died. What was he getting his hopes up for?

Don't cling to it, he told himself. *Don't think about stupid things.*

It would be foolish to have hope. Indeed. He must have been an incredible fool. If he were clever, this never would have happened.

"Depending on her state, are you saying there's something that can be done...?"

"There's a way," Jessie responded immediately. Then, with a snort, he added, "Just one."

4 | My Precious Teacher and Him

WHEN HAD it started?

I really hated coming back to the house.

When I stood in front of the door, I suddenly felt like I was being shut away in a stupidly narrow place, and it made me nauseous.

Had it always been this way? That couldn't be right. When had it started? I didn't really know.

Anyway, I hated my house.

I had really wanted to sing today, so I'd invited some people along, gone for a karaoke session, extended it, and extended it, and extended it. One person had left, then another, then another. Once everyone had said they had to go home, I reluctantly ended it, but in the end, we were there a total of four hours. I generously footed the whole bill. I mean, I was the one who'd invited them, after all, right? While singing like crazy, I'd also been eating and drinking, so I wasn't hungry.

This time of day, someone was probably back already. The lights were on, too.

I took my key out of my bag and opened the lock. The door opened. I went inside.

The trick was to do this all in one motion. If I stopped partway through, I'd want to run away. Not that it'd help.

Even if I told everyone we should go somewhere after this, we'd just finished four hours of karaoke. Nobody was going to come with me. Playing by myself was no fun, either. Once in a while, it could be good. I'd gone to a game center alone today, after all.

The lights in the entrance lit up as the sensor picked up my movements. There were high-heeled shoes. My mother's shoes.

I took off my shoes and went into the house.

I climbed the stairs in the entrance hall up to the second floor. I went into my own room and turned on the lights. Throwing my bag down, and trying not to step on the objects scattered across the floor, I headed for the bed.

Without stripping off my uniform, I dove into bed and rolled over onto my back.

Looking idly at the posters on the ceiling, I thought, *Huh, when did I put those up again?*

There were all kinds of posters, from idol posters, to posters from manga magazines, to movie posters. After running out of space for them on the walls, I'd started posting them on the ceiling, too.

Pulling off my socks, I threw them away to land wherever. My right foot touched something. It was a tiny basketball. I grasped it with my feet, threw it up, and caught it with my hands. Sitting up, I aimed at the miniature basketball hoop in a corner of the room. I took the shot.

"All right! Go in...!"

The ball was mercilessly deflected by the hoop.

"Aaargh! What the hell! Enough of this!"

I got really mad, and decided to sleep it off.

Nah... I'd have loved to sleep, if I could have, but I wasn't able to yet.

"...Ahhh." I let my voice out for no reason.

I pulled on my hair.

"Urgh," I groaned.

I sighed.

I let my voice out. "Uhhh."

Then I changed my tone, and went, "Ehhh" instead.

Changed it up, and went, "Ohhh."

"Heh heh," I chuckled.

"...So bored."

Lying on my front, I pressed my face into my pillow. It smelled of hairstyling products, shampoo, and other things. It was by no means fragrant. But I didn't hate it. It wasn't good, but it wasn't bad.

Maybe this is what life's like, I suddenly thought.

"It could be... That might be how it is. Yeah. Damn, I'm cool. Whoa. My throat's dry..."

I got up and scratched my head. I should've stopped by the convenience store to buy drinks on my way back. But it was too much of a pain to go out again now. It looked like there was no choice.

"Guess I'm going downstairs..."

I got out of bed, left my room, and went down to the first floor. There was a narrow hall stretching from the entrance hall. The door on the left was the toilet, and the door at the end went to the living room.

When I opened the door, the TV was on. My mother was still in her outdoor clothes, sitting on the sofa and drinking something. That something was probably wine, as usual.

There was a ridiculously huge wine cellar in this house, and it housed close to a hundred bottles. Just about every night, my mother would drink wine out of a stupidly large wine glass.

My mother glanced over in my direction, then said nothing. If she had said anything, I'd have gotten mad, but being ignored was infuriating, too.

I passed through the living room to the kitchen, and dug through the refrigerator. "...Damn. Why does this house have nothing but carbonated water and mineral water? What is this crap? I can't believe this."

When I muttered that aloud without meaning to, I heard my mother click her tongue, and that rubbed me the wrong way.

"...What?" I demanded. "I didn't say anything that wasn't true. You got a problem with me?"

"Why are you so foul-mouthed? I don't know who you took after. It must have been your dad, though, I'm sure."

My mother was apparently drunk. That didn't mean I was obligated to shrug this off, though. I slammed the fridge door shut.

"By my 'dad,' I suppose you mean that husband of yours? Or is it someone else?"

"Huh? Someone else? What do you mean?" she asked.

"How should I know? You don't seem to like your husband much, so I figured maybe you're having an affair. Nah, not just now, maybe you had one before?"

"Don't talk nonsense."

"It's not nonsense. It's a fairly serious problem, you know. Am I the old man's kid?"

"Don't be stupid. But it's true, you don't look like your brother or sister. They're not rude like you are."

"You're saying Bro and Sis aren't like me, they're honor students, is that it? I figured."

"What? You're bitter now? The reason you're such a failure is you make no effort, isn't it? That's your own fault."

"I'm not bitter. Sure, I'm jealous of them, yeah. They left me alone in this crappy house, and got out as soon as they could. Like, what the hell? Seriously. Seriously."

"If you're going to say that, why don't you get out already, too?"

"You don't have to tell me that. Once I graduate from high school, I'm out of here."

"If you're so against sponging off your parents, why don't you drop out and get a job?"

"Wow, you're a piece of work. I haven't heard of many parents telling their kid to drop out of high school."

"If you don't want to be in this house, that's all. If you're going to play around with the money your parents earned, would you mind not complaining so much?"

I got so pissed off, I kicked the kitchen counter.

My mother shouted, "What are you doing?!"

"What d'ya think I'm doing?! I kicked the counter!"

"The way you take your anger out on things is just like him!"

"You're not making me happy here, you know?!"

"I'm not trying to make you happy!"

"It's my birthday, damn it...!"

Once I had said the words, I couldn't cover my mouth. It was too late.

Honestly, why had I said that? Obviously, I hadn't meant to. It didn't matter one bit that it was my birthday. It had nothing to do with this.

Besides, think about it. When was the last time we'd celebrated my birthday? When I was in elementary school? Third grade, maybe fourth? That had to be about it. The atmosphere in this house had been terrible for that long. And once my mother started working, things got even worse.

My father only came back home about twice a week. Even when he did, it was late at night. He probably had another house. My mother probably had a lover, too. Despite that, she came home every day.

I didn't know how many times I'd seen my mother and father fighting. It always mystified me. If they got along so poorly, why didn't they divorce?

My brother had gotten a job last year. My sister was in

university. Both of them never came around to the house anymore.

For my brother and sister, the way they saw it was apparently, *Well, it's between them as husband and wife. Let them do what they like. They're sending us money like they're supposed to.*

Well, sure, they could see it that way. For sure. When my brother found a job, my father bought him an expensive car, and when my sister had her coming-of-age ceremony, they ordered a wonderful kimono for her. When my father occasionally went to Tokyo on business trips, he ate sushi with my brother in Ginza. My sister kept in frequent contact with my mother.

Was it my father who bought my sister that ring from Tiffany's, or my mother? Well, it was one of the two.

I had no expectations of my parents. The thing was, I was receiving money. I had a dedicated account, and when the balance got low, whether it was because they were making deposits or for whatever other reason, it went up on its own.

I had never wanted for anything. That was enough. There was no need to expect anything from them.

Who cared about a birthday? It was just one day out of 365 in a year. Naturally, I hadn't told my friends today was my birthday, either. Even if they asked me, I wouldn't tell them.

What, you don't know my *birthday? Man, you're hopeless,* was about all the response I'd give them.

I made the effort to find out my pals' birthdays and to plan parties for them, though. Preparing little gifts for them and stuff. I mean, why not? It's basic human decency. I wasn't expecting anything in return, okay? I was only doing it because I felt like it.

Yeah, that didn't matter. Seriously, it didn't. Neither did the fact it was my birthday today.

"And?" My mother looked even closer to snapping, for some reason.

Whew. Was she going to blow up at me, when I was the one who ought to be mad? Knocking back her glass, she kept the wine in her mouth for a moment. Then, she swallowed. I couldn't stand the way she drank.

"And...nothing, really," I muttered.

"If it's money you want, I'm already giving it to you, aren't I? Why don't you go buy whatever-it-is you want?"

"That's not it...!"

"I know you won't be happy if I buy you something, so why is that a surprise?" she snarled.

"I never said I wanted you to buy me something, and I don't!"

"Well, what?! Your brother and sister texted me on my birthday, and even sent gifts, but you didn't even wish me a happy birthday, you know?! Isn't it a bit much to expect me to celebrate yours after that?! You don't do anything yourself, but then you complain I don't do this, or I don't do that! You're just like him! When I look at you, you make me sick!"

"Then be sick!" I screamed. "Puke, puke, puke your guts out! Gulp down your wine, and then puke it back up, you tramp!"

"How dare you...!"

Suddenly, my mother gagged. She dropped her glass, and clutched her mouth with both hands. She bent over on the sofa.

Oh, crap. I tried to look away quickly, but it was too late. I saw the decisive moment clearly.

"What are you doing, at your age?" I muttered.

I'd thought she was drinking a lot, but not that she'd actually had enough to throw up. It was enough to make me feel sick, too. If I wasn't careful, I'd get nauseous. If that happened, it wouldn't just be the worst. It'd be the absolute worst.

My mother must have given up, because she decided to let it all come up there. She leaned over the low table in front of the sofa, coughing and sputtering.

I should've left that tramp and gone back to my room. Despite that, the next thing I knew, I was fetching a box of tissues and chucking it to my mother.

"...Thanks," my mother said awkwardly in a quiet voice, and began wiping her hands and face.

Gross. This was seriously pathetic. I'd never liked my mother, but this was the first time I'd ever felt such strong contempt for her.

"A cloth..." I started to say, then closed my mouth. But my mother had apparently already heard me.

"In the changing room, beneath the sink..."

"Yeah, whatever."

I wasn't rushing, but I headed to the bathroom with long, quick strides, and opened the doors to the cupboard beneath the sink. Buckets, cloths, and cleaning supplies. I tried to put water in a bucket, but the faucet was in the way, and I couldn't put it in the sink.

"What, I have to use the bath...?"

With no alternative, I used the shower to fill up the bucket, and threw the cloth into it. When I brought the bucket to the living room with some soap, my mother said, "I'm sorry."

What exactly was she apologizing for? I wanted to ask, but I didn't want to know the answer.

I left the bucket and soap, went back to my room, killed the lights, and jumped into bed. Once I had gotten under the covers, I took off my uniform, leaving myself in nothing but a T-shirt and underwear.

I turned to the side and curled into a ball. I was calmest when I was in this position, with my right arm between my legs and my left arm holding my knees.

It was my birthday, though, I wanted to mutter.

Seriously, what a laugh.

My old man had a natural wave, but my big bro and big sis weren't even slightly curly. My mom's hair, by the way, was dead straight. Of three siblings, I was the only curly one. I took after my old man.

But my old man, I was sure he hated me. He'd never praised me, not even once. But I could remember a load of times he'd gotten mad.

Lately, he didn't even get mad at me. I rarely even met him. It might have been less that he hated me, and more he didn't care.

My big bro and big sis didn't think about me, either. Even though it was my birthday, they hadn't texted me.

I had friends. Lots of friends. I was always popular, y'know? Never had a shortage of people to play with.

If I said I'd pay, everyone came along. If I hadn't paid? Who knows? They were used to it, you know. Having me treat them. They weren't going to grow up to be decent adults.

They were trash. Yeah, trash. Nothing but trash.

Trash. Trash. Trash. Trash. Trash. Trash. Trash. Trash.

This was a trashy world, full of nothing but trash covered in trash.

Ugh, I didn't care anymore. Nothing mattered. Maybe I was better off just staying here like this forever. I liked narrow spaces, anyway.

Being alone wasn't bad. Everyone else was trash, after all. Nothing but trash.

Come on, text me, at least. It was my birthday today.

Yeah, what did that matter? It didn't. It had nothing to do with this. It didn't mean a thing. Damn, I was tired. Like, seriously, so ti...

"...Uh?" Ranta murmured, rubbing his eyes.

For a bit, just now...had he fallen asleep?

"Seriously?" he muttered.

He didn't remember what it was about, but he felt like he'd had a dream. Probably not a very good one.

Man, I've got some guts, he thought with a stifled laugh.

Ranta was in a tree.

To describe the tree by comparison, it was like tens... no, hundreds of snakes had intertwined, supporting each other as they reached for the skies. Ranta was lying low with his back to it.

Of course, he wasn't doing that to kill time, or play around. Obviously. Ranta thought it was important to always maintain a sense of playfulness, but considering the fact that the guy chasing him, old man Takasagi, was a concrete threat and was bearing down on him, he couldn't afford that now.

That being the case, when Takasagi's voice had gotten gradually closer, Ranta had sensed he was in trouble, left his hiding place in the shadow of the tree, and gone inside it instead.

The tree trunk that was like hundreds of intertwined snakes didn't just look like that; it was actually made up of many thin trunks. Thanks to that, with some searching, he found a gap. It looked like he could get inside.

He was aware it was a dangerous gamble. From outside the tree, Ranta probably wasn't visible. In the same way, he couldn't see outside of the tree, so he was forced to guess at the situation based on sounds.

It had taken some work to get inside, so the same would likely be true on the way out. That meant if Takasagi sniffed out his location, he couldn't get away.

His heart was pounding, to say the least.

The old man was constantly shouting, "Ranta! Rantaaaaa!"

The old man's voice was getting closer, too.

Honestly, you know what? I'm kinda maybe thinking I may have screwed up.

Yeah. Well, sure? If you were to ask if he was really thinking that, he wasn't really, or maybe he was just a little bit, but maybe not. That'd be defeatist, you know? This was a man who never doubted he'd succeed, okay? What good would it do him to think about what'd happen if he failed? He'd cross that bridge when he came to it. He was a rare man with wisdom, bravery, and nobility all in one package, after all...

He wasn't afraid. Not one bit. That could be said definitively.

As proof, Ranta didn't budge an inch when right over there— it was hard to say exactly how far, but it was probably really close—he heard Takasagi's voice yelling, "Rantaaa!"

He held his breath and stayed put. Was he scared out of his wits, you ask? No, no, no. That wasn't it at all, okay? He was convinced he'd be fine, all right? It was all smooth sailing from here, after all, y'know? Man. Seriously.

I wish I could show you all how calm and self-possessed Ranta was then, he thought, smirking. *To show the whole world, and announce it for all to hear. Like, 'Here is the great Ranta-sama, mightiest of all dread knights!'*

Whatever the case, since he couldn't run away, he had to keep quiet. He was honestly and truly prepared for that.

But I obviously wasn't expecting to fall asleep, okay...?

Now then.

How long was I out for?

Exactly how many minutes had passed since he heard

Takasagi's voice exceptionally close to him? Tens of minutes? Or a few hours?

He thought about it, but—

Yeah, I dunno. How would I know? Like, about the length of time and stuff. But I should hold out for a while, right? This is the time to be patient, right? The old man could still be nearby, after all, right? If he's right there, I'd be in trouble, after all, right? Like, a crazy amount of trouble. Patience, patience. The tree. Become a part of the tree. No, become the tree itself. I am a tree. Tree. So tree. No matter how you look at me, there's nothing but tree. The treeiest tree. Perfectly tree...

He...tried to be patient, you know?

I'm being patient.

But, still...

It's tough.

This is suffering.

What is this? Training?

Meditation?

Am I a monk?

Why would I be a monk? I'm no holy man. That makes no sense. But seriously?

I wanna take a piss.

Taking a leak here was probably no good. He might have to consider it in a worst case scenario, though. It went without saying that Ranta-sama was a realist, and if push came to shrub... Er, no, if push came to shrug... No, push came to shove, he wouldn't be adverse to doing it, but right now, was it so bad he just had to go? Was this a crisis situation? Was the end of the world near? No, not really...?

Let me come out and say it. A man cannot win against his bladder. This is the truth.

Well, he had his ears wide like saucers—only not, because you don't open your ears wide like saucers, you do that with your eyes— but setting aside whether one's ears can be like saucers, he'd had his ears perked up while he was holding his bladder, and he'd heard nothing that indicated anyone was nearby, so it was probably fine.

Takasagi had certainly passed through here. However, he was no longer nearby. Just like the end of the world, Takasagi was not near.

No one had any right to complain if he came to that conclusion. Like, he couldn't hold it in. He couldn't. He had to piss, piss, piss, piss, damn it. If he didn't, he was going to turn into a piss demon. He could beg for help, but no one was going to help him, so he'd just have to do something about his piss himself.

Basically, I'm gonna do it!

It's the only option! That's all!

Pushing through the flexible trunks, or branches, or whatever they were, he jumped out into the world outside. Naturally, he looked around, and confirmed that there was no one around.

Look, look, look, see? No one was there, okay? Just like he'd thought, right? Which meant, basically, it was just as planned, wasn't it? Damn, he was going to burst.

No, calm down, don't panic, he told himself. He hummed something as he relaxedly, but quickly, dropped his pants, and...

"Ah..."

His voice leaked out.

This feeling of R-E-L-E-A-S-E...

But, wow, was it coming out. It sure was. It was splurting out. Had he held back this much?

Thinking about it, he hadn't gone in forever, so he had to have been holding it in for a fair bit, but could this much urine fit inside a single person? How about it? This volume of piss. Wasn't it weird? It was hard to believe it was all his own. Was his urinary tract connected to somewhere else, maybe? Like, was there a tank with ten people's worth of urine in it there? He suspected that, in truth, this urine was coming from there...

"Ooh..."

He shuddered.

It looked like it was all out.

Ranta forgot to put his thing back in his pants as he let out the deepest sigh ever.

This sense of achievement, it was nothing to make light of.

Like, I dunno. Maybe I was born for this moment? And thus, I'll begin walking forward once more to create my legend?

To engage in a bit of hyperbole, at that moment, Ranta was basking in a feeling like he had become an all-knowing, all-powerful god. Everything would work out, and nothing was impossible. He believed that, so when he suddenly heard his name being called, he never expected it.

"Ranta!"

That was why it didn't feel real, and Ranta turned around slowly.

He came out of the shadow of a tree maybe ten meters ahead.

"That's where you were, huh?" the one-eyed, one-armed man said.

Ranta's first thought was, *That oughta be my line,* or something like that, but he couldn't get the words out. Instead, something like a hiccup came out. "Urp..."

Takasagi stopped walking and frowned. "Hey." He gestured to him with his chin.

With that, Ranta finally responded, "...Yes, sir."

What am I saying, "Yes, sir," for? We're not a teacher and student, he thought, strongly embarrassed for a moment.

When he thought about it, though, their relationship hadn't been entirely unlike that of a master and apprentice for a short while.

Well, maybe it's fine, then, he thought. *Yeah, no, it isn't. I dunno? Hm. Which is it...?*

"For now, do something about that thing," the old man said.

"...What thing?"

"Don't tell me you came out of hiding to take a piss."

"Ah...!"

Ranta realized his thing was still hanging free and loose, and hurriedly stuffed it in his pants. In a fluster, he drew RIPer and got into a stance.

Takasagi showed no sign of even placing his hand on his katana's sheath. What was he seeing with that right eye of his? What exactly was this man thinking? His face seemed to say, *Maybe it's time for a smoke,* but that clearly couldn't be it.

Whew. Ranta took a breath. His body was shrinking away. *You can't move like this. That old man's going to one-shot you. Keep it together, me,* he warned himself. *Or should you relax instead? Hard to say. Hold on, how could you possibly relax, you idiot?!*

The distance between him and Takasagi was about seven meters. Should he close the distance with Leap Out and go for a surprise attack? No way, no way, no way. This wasn't an opponent that would work on.

Was Takasagi alone? Did he have allies? He'd have liked to look around, but it was dangerous to take his eyes off Takasagi now. Too dangerous. It would practically be suicide. Seriously, seriously, this old man was just too crazy. It was ridiculous.

Ranta was immediately sweating.

"Let me just say..." Takasagi sighed. He twisted his neck, and there was a cracking sound from the joint. That noise made Ranta jump, and he felt a burning shame in his chest from that fact.

"...Wh-wh-what?"

"You don't stand a one-in-a-million chance of beating me now."

"I-if it's a one-in-a-million chance, it's worth trying, at least..."

"I said you don't even have that one-in-a-million."

"You don't know that! Not until I try it!"

"Then try it. I'll take you on."

Takasagi drew his katana with ease.

His left arm hung limply, and the tip of his sword was almost touching the ground.

Even I know, Ranta thought, clenching his teeth. *I'm not an idiot. I'm well aware you're not an opponent I can beat.*

What was the difference in their abilities?

If Ranta was level 50, Takasagi was level 99…

Huh? Level? What kind of level? Well, combat level, or something like that? Whatever the case, even if he wasn't twice as powerful, Takasagi was close to twice as powerful. That was a pretty big gap. To give an example, Ranta was around 170 centimeters tall, so double that would come to a little over 340 centimeters. If he fought a guy like that, his chance of winning was zero.

Were there any openings he could take advantage of?

Fundamentally, there were none.

This man never missed a trick, after all. If it looked like there was an opening, that was instead reason for caution, and it was best to assume it was a trap.

How was this one-armed, one-eyed, middle-aged man so powerful?

If only for a short time, Takasagi had trained Ranta like a master would a disciple. So, of course, Ranta had thought about this in his own way. Where was the secret to Takasagi's power?

In terms of his athletic abilities, they probably weren't above average. That meant he wasn't exceptionally fast or strong. For endurance, he wasn't young anymore, so he should have been past his peak. Was it experience? He had that, naturally. But that surely couldn't be all there was to it.

It wasn't just Takasagi. There was one thing that all strong guys tended to have in common, and that was grit. If there was one thing about strong guys, above all else, well, it was that nothing shook them. Even if they were in a crisis where they ought to think, *I'm totally screwed now. I'm absolutely gonna die,* they were totally calm, weren't they? They had the guts it took to be able to be like that.

Were all tough guys dense? Did they not feel scared, or threatened?

That probably wasn't it. If that were the case, they'd just be idiots.

It wasn't that they weren't afraid, it was that they knew acting scared wouldn't do any good, and they dealt with the threat with the proper recognition that it was a threat. That was it, right?

Takasagi was scary. Super scary. So scary that, even though he'd already taken a piss, Ranta might wet himself. When he had an enemy that scary in front of him, what could he do?

He stopped sweating.

His breathing had been ragged all this time, but now Ranta was breathing normally.

Takasagi's lips curled upward on one side.

"Yeah. That's good."

Does he think he's my teacher or something?

No, if I get mad, things won't be any different from before. I have to look at things as they are, and accept them. I don't know what Takasagi's after, and it doesn't matter. There's lots I can learn from Takasagi. That's the key thing.

"So, what next, Sensei?" Ranta asked.

Takasagi's one eye narrowed a little. "I'm not much of a verbal teacher. You'll have to learn as we go."

"Oh yeah? Well, okay then." Ranta jumped straight backwards. "That suits me better, too!"

Exhaust. To an onlooker, it might seem like he was just jumping, but it was actually different. When an ordinary person tried to jump high or far without a running start, they would bend their knees and crouch, then quickly stretch out their knees to leap. Dread knights didn't do that. They used a special method to not so much bend as twist their ankles, knees, and waists, which instantly created an explosive burst of power.

In addition, by kicking the ground with their heels and toes in alternation, they could increase their propulsion. This special technique called the Shadow Step was, in a way, the thing that made a dread knight a dread knight. It used leg muscles that weren't usually used, so it couldn't be learned just by watching, and it was likely only a dread knight would know precisely how it worked.

Because of Shadow Step, a dread knight's calves were unusually developed, and misshapen. Furthermore, using Shadow Step not only polished their movement skills like Exhaust, Leap Out, and Missing, but it also lent a sharp edge to various attack skills like Hatred.

The difference in power between them was beyond obvious, but Takasagi wasn't a dread knight. There were things Ranta the dread knight could do that Takasagi couldn't.

If Ranta had one thing in which he held the advantage over Takasagi, it was this: the fact he was a dread knight.

"Are you all talk, Ranta...?!"

Takasagi immediately came after him.

For a middle-aged guy, he was ridiculously fast on the start up. That said, he wasn't as good as a dread knight's Exhaust.

Without a word, Ranta used Exhaust a second, then a third time, and put even more distance between him and Takasagi. If he could keep using Exhaust forever, it would be possible to escape like this. However, obviously, that was impossible. Thousand Valley had a lot of obstacles like trees, and the ground wasn't level.

While he was in the middle of making his fourth Exhaust with Shadow Step while avoiding hitting any trees, he nearly got his foot snagged on a dead branch. He couldn't afford to fall over. Stumbling a little, Ranta came to a stop.

Takasagi closed in. He was still more than ten meters away. Well, it was probably twelve, maybe thirteen meters. Ranta had a lot of room to work with.

"So long, old man...!"

Ranta turned his back on Takasagi. If this were a pure game of tag, Ranta being the younger of the two, he wouldn't lose.

Besides, he had a twelve-meter head start, so he could run away. Make it look like he was going to fight, then book it out of there. This was very much the sort of thing Ranta would do. It was a common but effective move.

While confirming the locations of the trees, Ranta ran for twenty meters.

The distance between him and Takasagi was hardly changed.

What about the guys from Forgan? For now, he didn't see any. Were they not around here?

Is it about time?

The moment he thought that, Ranta leapt backwards with Exhaust without hesitating.

Twisting his body in midair, he used Leap Out. He sprang at Takasagi.

Takasagi...laughed.

Laugh. Laugh all you want.

Ranta swung RIPer down diagonally.

Hatred. It was a strike with speed and all his strength behind it, but Takasagi's katana easily brushed it aside. Ranta was being treated like a child.

Of course. *I knew I would be.*

Ranta immediately retreated with Exhaust. Then he used Missing. With this skill, to describe it in the broadest terms, he swung his upper body left or right, then jumped in the opposite direction. Most people relied on their vision, and that made it easy to trick them with what they saw. The opponent would be caught on the dread knight's motion, and they'd look in the direction his upper body swung despite themselves. However, the dread knight would actually move the opposite way, so it would feel like they lost sight of him for an instant.

However, Takasagi wasn't deceived. His one eye was firmly fixated on Ranta.

It meant a trick like this wouldn't work on a battle-hardened veteran like him.

It was good to have that made clear, if nothing else. Takasagi seemed like he'd be good at outfoxing his opponents, after all. Ranta had no intention of fighting him that way.

Ranta used Leap Out diagonally to the left. He got seven to eight meters away from Takasagi.

Takasagi didn't move. He was waiting. He saw through it, was that it?

I'm impressed, old man. But I'm not backing down just because you can read me. I'm gonna do this.

From Exhaust, he twisted his body and did a Leap Out. It was the same attack as before, but this time he didn't swing down with RIPer.

He thrust.

Anger.

Takasagi didn't block with his katana. He smoothly dodged to the left.

Here it comes. A counterattack, huh?

Ranta used Missing to make it look like he was going left, then jumped to the right.

Takasagi didn't bring his katana out. It looked like he'd hesitated, but who knew? The movement of his upper body with Missing should have had an even stronger effect at close range, so maybe even Takasagi had gone, *Oh!*

Could he use this?

He was going to test it.

Even if he kept calm, and used all his strength and ability as a matter of course, that wasn't going to be enough on its own. Ranta's power was far from being on par with Takasagi's, so he needed a little something extra.

He used Exhaust and Leap Out again to gain some distance,

then twisted and used Exhaust and Leap Out to spring towards Takasagi.

Ranta took the position for Hatred. The range was the same as for Hatred, too.

Takasagi was getting ready to block with his katana. Maybe this time instead of turning it aside, he'd knock it back.

Before that, Ranta used Missing to make it look like he was going left, then jumped to the right while swinging his sword.

It looked like he'd managed to surprise Takasagi. He backed away to avoid Ranta's sword.

"Interesting."

Oh yeah? This is interesting for you, old man? Well, I'm just getting started, he thought, but he didn't say it. It took a fair bit of perseverance to fight without talking. But Ranta had to do it.

He used Exhaust and Leap Out to get away from Takasagi.

Remove anything unnecessary.

He'd finally started to understand.

I wasn't serious at all. I want to get strong. I'm going to get strong. I'll definitely do it. I was all talk. I might have thought I was giving it my all, but it wasn't nearly enough.

Well, yeah? When there was a crisis, I was always as serious as could be. But that's true for anyone. No matter how easygoing of a fool you are, you get desperate when things are bad. I was only doing what anyone would, but I got full of myself, thinking I was doing things the right way.

I was naive.

In the end, I was complacent.

There has to be more I could have done, but I didn't.

So, what did I do?

I blamed others.

"I'm doing what I ought to just fine, so what's the problem with you guys? You're a bunch of trash without a shred of talent, aren't you? Well, I guess I can't blame you. In the end, we were just the left-overs. We're a bunch of small fry. I'm different, though, you know? I mean, I knew that from the start. I see all sorts of things. I never expected anything from you people to begin with, okay? Just do your best. But either way, if we succeed, it'll be thanks to me, and if we fail, it'll be your fault. Haruhiro. You especially. It's your fault for being leader when you have no aptitude for it. Isn't the reason we're in this sad state because you mess up every little thing? If this is all you people can do, then why should I be any better?"

It's not that I was actually thinking that way, Ranta thought. *But part of me was looking at you guys with a sense of detachment. Even if you people do everything you can with the one life you get, there are limits to what you can do. I mean, look at you.*

I'm different. Because I'm with you guys, I can't seem to move up in the world, but if I joined a better party, I'd work crazy hard and achieve super amazing things. I'm a man that Renji himself recognized, all right? I'm made of different stuff from the rest of you. Different stuff.

Though he'd believed that, on the other hand, he'd probably felt uncertain.

Ranta twisted, used Exhaust and Leap Out, and closed in on Takasagi. This time, it was Anger.

Takasagi put his weight on his right leg, and raised his katana slightly. That said, the tip was still lower than his waist. It was a defensive, lower position. He was watching to see what Ranta would do. Takasagi had gotten cautious. Ranta had made him raise his guard.

But don't get happy, he told himself. *Don't let it go to your head.*

Ranta didn't unleash Anger. Instead, he used Missing at the last moment. Made it look like he was going right, then jumped left. But he didn't swing his sword. Takasagi was following Ranta with his eyes just fine. His katana wasn't moving an inch.

Well, how about this, then?

Here he used Missing once more.

Takasagi raised his katana slightly.

Ranta attacked Takasagi with Hatred.

Takasagi's katana collided with RIPer, and sparks flew.

When their blades almost locked, Ranta used Reject. Using his wrists, elbows, shoulders, waist, and even his legs, he knocked his opponent away.

Takasagi only stepped back once before managing to hold his ground. He came at Ranta.

Ranta used Exhaust to head backwards. Exhaust. Exhaust.

Takasagi didn't pursue.

Whew. He took a breath and loosened up. *I have potential— or I ought to.*

But, seriously, seriously, is this all the ability I have?

Is the real me stronger?

Is the reason I can't bring out my power because I hang out with a bunch of small fry?

But still.

If I pushed myself to my limit of limits, where I couldn't possibly do any more, doing training or whatever, and this was all I amounted to, I'd be beyond shocked.

Even I know it. Shouting all the time in the middle of combat is pointless. I think of all these special attack names, but they aren't that special in the end. Haruhiro and the rest are seriously, seriously pushing close to their limits, and I'm actually getting saved by them, I know. But that's not my style, is it? Focusing on just one thing like an idiot and keeping at it. Taking forever thinking about this and that. I'm me, and they aren't serious about trying to stop me, so what's the harm?

I have power to spare. I've got room to grow still. This is easy for me. Easy. What're they getting so serious about? They're too serious, man. What a bunch of killjoys. I'm not kidding, they are.

You guys are always so serious, and it's lame. That's not cool, okay? I mean—

I mean, you struggle your hardest, get covered in blood and mud, keep struggling, and if that doesn't work, what then...?

"I can't get along with those guys," I thought. "Our philosophies are different. Our beliefs don't match up. There's a difference in the way they think and I think. In the end, we're a poor match. That's not where I belong." But, well, keeping with something because I already started it? That's a thing. I toughed it out and managed to make it this far.

But eventually our roads were going to diverge. I was always going to part ways with those guys. Because it had to be out there somewhere. The place I belong. Guys I could like from the bottom of my heart. They'd value me properly, and I'd respect them, too.

The reason I'm like this, Haruhiro, it's your fault.

It's not my fault. I wasn't wrong. I'm not weak.

I'm a heel. Everyone hates me. That's fine. It doesn't bother me in the least. That sort of role is actually easier to play, you know.

I don't need to be liked. If I accept that, I don't need to pay attention to your needs. I don't need to contort myself. I can do as I please. Yeah, say whatever you like. No matter what you guys think, I'm fine, dammit .

"Rantaaa."

Takasagi raised his katana. The left hand that was gripping the hilt of his katana was near his chin. The blade was inclined a bit to Ranta's right. His left foot was forward. His knees were bent, and his hips lowered.

Ranta didn't know much about how a katana was used, so he was working on speculation, but that was probably a combined offensive and defensive stance.

Next time, at the very beginning…in other words, when Ranta tried to attack, he meant to crush him. Never letting him get started, so to speak. Takasagi had seen enough of Ranta's movements, and he'd gotten a grip on them. At the very least, that was what Takasagi had decided.

…He thinks he can underestimate me.

Let's do this!

If you think you can stop me, you can damn well try!

If Ranta had been the same as he'd been up until now, he'd

have let the blood rush to his head and charged at Takasagi like that. That'd be showing no growth whatsoever.

He was eight meters from Takasagi. Ranta deliberately came to a stop.

"...Huh?" Takasagi frowned slightly.

Don't worry. I haven't gotten cold feet. I'm a dread knight.

He could fight as a dread knight. It was his one advantage.

And a dread knight had more than just their dread martial arts.

"O Darkness—"

When Ranta tried to cast his spell, Takasagi charged. Ranta somehow managed to keep chanting without losing his concentration.

"O Lord of Vice, Demon Call."

"You dog of Skullhell...!" Takasagi's katana stretched out. It wasn't a slash or a thrust. It was like Takasagi's arm had merged with his katana to become a whip.

It was a close call. If he was even a moment slower in backing away with Shadow Step, Ranta would have fallen victim to Takasagi's katana. If he had panicked and run away even a little sooner, even if he managed to keep chanting as he fled, the spell might not have been completed.

In the spot Ranta had been a moment before, right behind Takasagi, a blackish purple cloud-like thing had appeared. The cloud rapidly formed a vortex.

Inhaling sharply, Takasagi began to turn, then leapt to the side.

The cloud was already taking on a familiar shape. It could be described as like a human with a purple sheet over its head, carrying a knife in its right hand and a club-like weapon in its left. Despite floating, it had two proper legs, and that made it feel strange and uncanny. Its two eyes were like holes, and beneath them was a gash-like maw.

Its name was Zodiac-kun.

The dread knight Ranta's demon.

"Hehe... hahahahaha...! Long time no see, worthless Ranta...! Go die ten thousand times right now...!"

"No—" Takasagi took a sharp swing with his sword. "You die!"

Zodiac-kun did a floating backflip to avoid Takasagi's slash. "Hehe... hahaha... You want to die before Ranta, geezer...?"

"I'm not a geezer! I'm barely middle-aged!"

Takasagi went at Zodiac-kun. He was uncharacteristically worked up.

Zodiac-kun slipped backwards, getting away from Takasagi. Zodiac-kun would then do yet another floating backflip, or twist around to avoid Takasagi's katana.

While catching his breath, Ranta watched Takasagi. Would someone like the old man snap that easily? He didn't know. It could have been a ruse, or he might have been sensitive about how he was aging, and gotten angry despite himself. Ranta couldn't tell which it was.

Takasagi was a good actor. He didn't reveal what was in his heart so easily. Did that mean he was acting, after all? He was luring Ranta in? Or maybe Takasagi's goal was to confuse Ranta?

Every move he makes has some intention.

This is a battle, huh?

I have to use my head to the max like this?

What a pain. I can't do this. I'll settle this quickly, in one go. I'm going to say goodbye to the old me that thought that way, right?

"O Darkness, O Lord of Vice, Dread Venom!" Ranta called forth a dark miasma, and tried to engulf Takasagi in it.

Takasagi ran from the miasma, and from Zodiac-kun. He raced with a swiftness you wouldn't expect from a middle-aged man, and ran away. The miasma had little ability to trace him. However, Ranta had predicted the direction Takasagi would retreat.

Ranta used Leap Out to jump in the direction Takasagi was going, and used Slice. He swung RIPer in a figure-eight shape. No, halfway through the eight, Ranta's sword was knocked away by Takasagi's katana.

"Hehe...!" Zodiac-kun caught up to Takasagi, and was swinging down with the knife-like weapon.

That was when Takasagi did something awesome. He likely swung his katana down diagonally as he turned, then immediately, without stopping, turned again and swung his katana up.

Zodiac-kun somehow blocked with the knife-like weapon, and Ranta blocked with his sword, but—Ranta landed on his backside, his hands were numb, and he had come close to dropping his sword, while Zodiac-kun was sent flying five or six meters.

What power.

I could barely see it, too. That was devilishly fast now, you know...?

No, now wasn't the time to be surprised. Ranta bent over and used Exhaust. He put some distance between him and Takasagi.

Dammit...

Screw you, old man.

"So you *can* do it if you try, Rantaaa." Takasagi boastfully tapped the flat side of his katana on his own left shoulder, and gave Ranta a lopsided grin.

This is easy for you, is that it?

Yeah, that figured. Just now, Takasagi had given Ranta a pass. While Ranta was flat on his butt, he should have been able to bisect him if he'd so desired. He'd deliberately chosen not to.

Takasagi let out a throaty chuckle. "You just died once."

Why? Why didn't he kill me? Is he trying to make me owe him? Is he seriously still playing teacher, or something? Screw you. Screw you to death.

"...Yeah."

Ranta accepted it all.

Zodiac-kun was looking this way, but not providing any of the verbal abuse that was the demon's specialty. In the depths of his hole-like eyes, something flashed—or maybe Ranta just imagined it.

"You're right." Ranta recognized it, then sighed. "But I'm not dead. That means I can keep fighting with you."

"Not so much." Takasagi shrugged and sniffled. He looked down. He then immediately raised his face, and fixed his one eye on Ranta.

"This is all I'm gonna say. We'll forgive you just this one time. The boss ain't mad. I dunno about the rest, but if I side with the boss, they'll fall in line. Come back with me, Ranta."

Ranta tried to open his mouth. But what was he supposed to say...?

I'm supposed to listen to you? Old man, is that how you really feel? You aren't trying to catch me by surprise, are you? You wouldn't do that, huh? You'd do it if you had to, sure, but not against me. Even without doing that, you can kill me. In that case...

You're serious?

You mean that for real?

You came all this way, not to kill me for stabbing you in the back, but to bring me back?

You'll forgive me?

Me, who basically spat in your face? I can be forgiven? I can go back to Forgan, you're saying? That's really...

Ranta blinked. Not once. He repeatedly blinked. He felt something building up in the back of his nose. His eyes were itchy. He came close to clicking his tongue. He gritted his teeth.

Don't do that.

Don't say that stuff to me.

I finally resolved to take off, and you're gonna hold me back.

"...I was at my limit," said Ranta.

Even if the old man said that, I shouldn't be saying this stuff. That's no good. Keep my mouth shut. I stabbed them in the back. It was a betrayal as clear as any, and I did it with a, "Ha, how'd you like that?"

No matter what I say now, it's just making excuses. That's fine. That's why I betrayed them that way. So that even if I wanted to go back, I couldn't.

"If I stayed with you guys any longer…I was going to become a member of Forgan, body and soul," said Ranta. "I felt like I was going to love you guys from the bottom of my heart. To live and die with you. I felt like I was going to start being okay with that, and not have a shred of doubt about it… That was my limit. I was at a crossroads. I had to make a choice. To become a member of Forgan, or…"

"Or what?"

"…To stay me."

"When you say 'me,' what do you mean?"

"Like… The me before I encountered you guys."

"The you who was wasting time, playing around with a bunch of brats you barely even knew?"

"It's not that I was playing around."

"Huh?"

"It might have looked to you like we were playing around. They were trying hard, in their own ways. We went through a lot, and some guys even died."

"If you're alive, everyone dies eventually. You and me, too. Even our boss, even though it feels like you could kill him and he still wouldn't stay dead. Even with Arnold the undead, if you split his head in two, he'll shut up for good. So what?"

"…I had a partner. I wasn't strong enough, and I let him die."

"You *let* him die? Big words there, Ranta. Are you that big a deal that you can shoulder the life and death of other people?"

"If I had it more together, he might not have died."

"No, that's wrong. The reason he died was because he wasn't

blessed with the fortune or personal power to struggle against his fate. That's how each and every one of us dies on his own."

"I'm sure you're right," Ranta said. "Old man, it's probably exactly as you say. If I stayed in Forgan, I'd eventually think like you. Even if you guys get along, you're not weirdly clingy. Everyone stands on his own feet. Even if you're hanging out with a bunch of like-minded guys, you know you'll be alone when you die. That's life. You guys are real men. You're cool, and I respect that. I want to be like you guys, too."

"Then be like us. Don't flinch over every little thing, and live boldly, whether that life is long or short. That's the kind of determination you need."

"It'd be a lie."

"What?"

"That's not the kind of person I am. I could stay in Forgan, and I could imitate you. I'm sure I'd enjoy that. But that's not who I really am."

"Word of advice from a middle-aged guy. Listen, Ranta. There's no such thing as a real you that exists out there somewhere. That doesn't just go for you. It goes for me, too. Don't think some path has been prepared in advance for either of us. If you see a road in front of you, it's an illusion. The road gets left behind you as you walk it. When you turn back and look at the footsteps behind you, that's who you are. One second later, they may turn in a completely different direction. That's you, too. The real you isn't something you search for and find. The way you live decides who you are. In other words, that is you."

"You sure can talk," Ranta laughed, but Takasagi smiled slightly, unabashed.

"I'm getting on in years, after all. I don't look it, though."

"You do look it, dammit ."

"I do, huh?"

"Yeah. I can tell you've lived twice as long as me. Honestly, what you're saying seeped in. Basically, you're saying no matter who I am, and who I've been, if I decide it, I can be anyone I want to be, right? If I want to live as a member of Forgan, I can do that..."

Ranta took a deep breath, then exhaled.

Takasagi said nothing. However, if Ranta kept quiet, Takasagi was going to have to push for an answer, or ask the question again.

Are you coming back?

He didn't want to let Takasagi say those words. It was only for a short time, but Takasagi really had trained Ranta like a teacher. Even now, he was teaching him things. Did he like doing that? Probably.

If he'd only had his skills going for him, he wouldn't be so trusted by the guys in Forgan, and wouldn't be in a position of authority and leadership. Jumbo might not be particular about it, but he was human, after all.

Was Takasagi looking after Ranta because they were both humans? That might be part of it. Either way, though, Takasagi had come to bring Ranta back.

Ranta was grateful.

He'd never thank him, though.

"In the beginning, I only became one of you to save my own skin, and to help that worthless woman," said Ranta. "It was only out of expedience. I thought I could get along with you guys, and I figured it wouldn't be bad to hang with you for a while, too. If I was in your ranks, I wouldn't have to think about every little thing, I could drink good booze, party, and have a fun and entertaining life and death. It was the best, dammit! It was so great, it made me sick! No matter what hell I've got to go through, I've got a reason I've gotta open Moguzo & Ranta's Ramen Shop! What reason, you ask?! Because I decided that's what I'm gonna do! I am! A dread kniiiiight...!"

He lost track of what he was even saying somewhere in the middle, but there was something seething inside him so hot it felt like it would gush out.

This was blood. Hot blood. Something he hadn't felt at any time he was with Forgan.

It was lukewarm then. I see. So that was it.

When I was with Parupiron and the rest, I was being too easy on myself, and that left me feeling lukewarm as a result. Even so, they were such a bunch of worthless losers that the situation was usually severe, and life and death crises were a near daily occurrence, so my blood ended up boiling on its own. However, when I tried to run away to Forgan, I was lukewarm again.

I could respect Jumbo, look up to Takasagi, and made friends with lots of people. Is that my path in life?

I say nay.

It was really appealing, and I'm sure it'd have felt good, but it's not what I, my magnificent self, seek from the depths of my heart and soul.

"Hehehe...!" Zodiac-kun suddenly let out an ominous laugh.

Takasagi tensed a little, then turned to face Zodiac-kun.

"Ehe...! Hehehehehehe...! Well said, Ranta...! Get cursed to death...!"

"You—"

Takasagi was speechless. Well, of course. Even the old man was going to be shocked.

I mean, even I'm at a loss here, okay?

Zodiac-kun was changing as they watched.

Wait, Zodiac-kun, that sheet-like thing... You actually were wearing it?

The sheet was now rolling up—or rather, peeling back—and a smooth figure that wasn't quite male or female, and was human-like—but clearly not human—appeared. It had a head—but no face! There were no eyes, or nose, or mouth.

Seriously? That's kind of gross, you know?

Though it was only for a second, he was able to see Zodiac-kun's naked body, which he had been curious about, but hadn't wanted to see. The sheet-like thing that had been peeled off the demon came apart and fell to pieces, turning into something like strings which wrapped around Zodiac-kun. In addition, the knife- and club-like weapons went *ba-bam* and turned into strings, too, taking new forms in Zodiac's hands.

"He... Hehehehehe... Hehehehehehehehehe... Hehehehe-hehehehehehehehe..."

This is crazy.

Seriously crazy.

My tears.

My runny nose.

Ranta shuddered.

There was someone with dark purple armor covering the entirety of their skinny body, leaving no gaps, and holding a long naginata-like pole arm with a heavily curved blade in both hands there.

The weapon's shape, the design of the armor... They couldn't have been more ominous, in a way that was indescribably amazing.

Yeah. That's the stuff.

Right?

That's the stuff, right?

If you're talking about dread knights, that's how it ought to be, right?

"...Damn cool," Ranta said.

"Ehe... Hehehehe... Praise me more... Die praising me..."

"No, hold on, Zodiac-kun—That's you?"

"Ehe... Hehehe... I demand a '-san,' you weak piece of crap..."

"Uh, okay, Zodiac-kun-san, then...?"

"..."

"Zodiac-san? Is that better?"

"..."

"Oh! How about we change your name to Zodie? Then I'll add a '-san,' making you Zodie-san."

"...-sama."

"Zodie-sama? 'Sama,' huh? Hm..." Ranta cocked his head to the side. "Yeah, about that '-sama.' Zodie-sama. It just doesn't sound right. It's not bad, though, I guess. How about Zodi-sama? Nah, no matter how I think about it, '-sama' just isn't right. Neither is '-san.' That said, you're my demon, right? Hold on, what're you going and evolving on your own for?! I haven't done any of that ritual stuff where I offer sacrifices to Skullhell to accumulate vice lately! I haven't done it in ages! I couldn't have even if I wanted to, though! I was praying in my heart, but we were in Darunngar , and then stuff happened!"

"The thing about that is..."

"Is what?"

"Heheh..."

Something like foxfire lit up in Zodie's eyes and flickered. That wasn't all. There was a faint air reminiscent of Dread Venom rising from the demon's whole body.

"It's a company secret... Ehe... Writhe and suffer until you eventually die..."

"But, no, you're not a company!"

"Skullhell is watching..."

"Huh?"

"I aaaam... Skulhellllll... The Daaaark Godddd..."

"N-no way! Skullhell?! The man himself?! You've manifested?! No, it's not 'the man,' I guess you're technically a god..."

"Teeeechnically...?!"

"S-sowwie! Not technically! You're a total god, God! I mean, damn, look at that divine aura! Hey, God! You're so godly! A god among gods! If you're not a god, Skullhell-sama, no one is!"

"Rage... Heh..."

"I-I'm sorry...!"

There was only one thing to do here.

The moment he had that flash of inspiration, his body was moving.

He leapt up, and contorted his whole body in midair. Then, landing so hard his head almost struck the ground, he got down on all fours and pressed his forehead into the dirt. It was his ultimate trump card.

THIS WAS THE KOWTOW!

NO!

THIS WAS THE JUMPING KOWTOOOOOOOW!

"I beg you...! Have forgiveness, Skullhell-sama!"

"Heheh... Heh..."

"I'll do anything, okay?! Maybe 'anything' is too much?! Erm, I'll give you anything short of my life. Well, honestly, I hope you'll let me off with just this show of my feelings, but I'll have to do whatever I can to compromise, really..."

"You don't seem...contrite enough... Ehehe..."

"Y-you think?! I-I don't think so, though! Hey, old man, you agree with me, right?!"

"You're throwing the conversation over to me?" Takasagi said incredulously. "How shameless are you?"

"You can see, can't you? I'm this shameless, okay?!"

"I have no words..."

"You're going to abandon me?! You coward!"

"Seriously, what am I supposed to say...?"

"Think for yourself, stupid! Whoops, that was a little far just now. Sorry, sorry." Ranta laughed, stood up, and held RIPer at the ready. "Okaaaay, I dunno how it happened, but the way I went around killing all sorts of stuff in a dread knight-y way must have made me rank up, or level up, or power up my Zodie! Now, let's do the dread knight-y thing and heinously double team the old man!"

"You're a natural piece of trash, aren't you?" Takasagi had a look of exasperation on his face.

It wasn't just that his body was not tensed; he even looked relaxed. Maybe it wasn't just a lack of tension; maybe his guard was down, too. If so, great.

Zodie, who was possessed by Skullhell—but not really, the demon had only been doing that as a comedy bit—spun the vicious-looking long naginata around once, then slowly approached Takasagi.

"O Darkness, O Lord of Vice... Dread Aura." Ranta immediately called forth a blackish purple air and wreathed himself in it.

This air was Skullhell's favorite given form, and it boosted a dread knight's physical abilities, and that increased with the amount of vice accumulated. Ranta had, at some point, accumulated enough vice to make Zodiac-kun evolve into Zodie.

I'm in top shape.

My body's light. It feels like my weight dropped by half.

Man, this is awesome.

My power is overflowing!

I feel like I'm gonna have a nosebleed.

Even so, he couldn't let it go to his head. He was quick to get carried away and get tripped up. It was a bad habit of Ranta's. No matter how hot his soul burned, he had to keep his head cool.

If he was honest with himself, he wanted to shout. To let out a loud war cry. But he wouldn't. Not because it was pointless. Because it would be a negative.

Takasagi glanced at Ranta, then at Zodie. There was a little tension in Takasagi's left arm as he swung his katana. Lowering his jaw, he placed himself on a straight line between Ranta and Zodie. Takasagi didn't face Ranta or Zodie, and he didn't turn his back to them, either.

Have at him! Ranta gave the order, and Zodie moved.

There was no sign remaining of the time when Zodie had been the adorable Zodiac-kun. At the same time, he could see a representation of himself in the demon, and he was already forming an attachment. However, a demon was only a demon. It might be fine to anthropomorphize it and adore it in his spare time, but he had to use it efficiently in battle.

Be heartless, Ranta told himself. *No, it's a mistake to show affection for a demon in the first place.*

"Heeeeeeeeeeeeeeeeeeeeeeeeeeeeeeeee...!" Zodie swung its long naginata at Takasagi.

Ranta jumped with Leap Out, too. But not straight forward. He tried to get around behind Takasagi's back. Takasagi would have wanted to prevent that, but Zodie was there.

Takasagi's katana knocked back Zodie's long naginata.

Zodie used the momentum from being pushed back to spin the naginata around, and took another swing like that.

Takasagi jumped back to the left diagonally. That's where Ranta attacked him.

Anger.

Takasagi twisted himself out of the way of Ranta's sword.

Then, the next thing he knew, there was a counterattack.

Takasagi swung his katana with something like a backhand attack, so it was hard for Ranta to predict. If his body hadn't been sharpened by Dread Aura, he probably wouldn't have been able to react and dodge it so quickly.

Ranta was still thrown off balance, and barely managed to escape with Leap Out. Takasagi wasn't able to follow and attack him.

"Eeeeeeeee...! Eeeeeee...! Eeeeeeeeeeeeeeee...!"

Zodie swung down its long naginata. Thrust, thrust, it kept attacking Takasagi.

Takasagi didn't block with his katana. He avoided the long naginata with ease. However, he didn't ignore Zodie and go after Ranta. He couldn't do it.

Zodie wasn't going in for the kill with Takasagi. There was no way Zodie could beat Takasagi alone, so the demon put him in check, keeping him pinned down, and focused only on doing that. No, that was what Ranta was having the demon do.

That said, even if he had Zodie focus entirely on the tank role, it wouldn't last long. Takasagi would see through Zodie's attacks soon. When that happened, Zodie was going down. In no time flat, probably.

Ranta twisted and chained an Exhaust with a Leap Out to charge at Takasagi.

Hatred.

Though Takasagi's breathing was frantic for a brief moment, he brushed Zodie's long naginata aside with his katana, and immediately turned to Ranta and—No. That wasn't it.

When the long naginata was swept aside, Zodie was wide open in front.

Takasagi stepped inside the demon's reach, tackled Zodie, and pushed it down. Then, turning back towards Ranta, he swung his katana diagonally.

When Takasagi tackled Zodie, Ranta wasn't expecting it, and he was already in mid-swing.

It felt like time was stretching out as Takasagi's katana closed in little by little. Ranta was trying to bend over backwards to avoid it, but he wasn't going to make it like this.

Why am I slow, too, not just the old man?! If we're both slow, there's no point.

His anger was misdirected. He knew that. Time had done nothing wrong. But why was it moving slowly to begin with? It seemed his head was moving faster on its own, and he had time to argue with himself about whether to do this or that. He could think all he liked, but if he couldn't move fast, it wasn't going to do him any good.

Takasagi's katana looked like it was going to bite into Ranta's chin.

He was almost there. If he could just bend his body a little more, he could dodge it by a hair's breadth.

He couldn't bend that little more.

If he gets a good cut in on the lower half of my head, it's gonna hurt like hell, and I won't be able to fight decently. With the enemy I'm facing being an experienced old man, that'll be the end, right?

No.

It's not over. I'm not going to die... Probably. I won't die.

In that case, I still have moves to make. Take the lightest wound I can manage, and fight back. I can do that, right?

Yeah, I can do it. I'm gonna do it. I'm a dread knight. I'm not scared of some old man. What dread knight has ever given up gracefully? Dread knights are stubborn to the point of pigheadedness, no question.

But... Huh?

That's weird.

Takasagi's katana has lost its edge. Maybe I can dodge this?

"Urk...!"

Ranta's body bent back all at once. His head impacted the ground.

Ow!

A bridge, right? That's what it's called, yeah? This position?

"Hungh...!" It went without saying he couldn't stay like this, so he used his head as a fulcrum and spun his whole body, picking up momentum, and jumped up. "Hoh...!"

Having missed, Takasagi clicked his tongue with an awkward look on his face, and then he took a thrust with his katana. "Argh...!"

That's not like you, old man.

Ranta shouted and hit Takasagi's katana aside, then took a slash at him. Takasagi blocked this with his katana. Then, before their blades could lock, he adjusted the angle of his blade and pushed.

Takasagi wanted to get away. He didn't want to lock blades. If that was the case, Ranta would cling on.

"Ungh...! Rah...!" Ranta's voice leaked out on its own.

Takasagi was a sly old fox. He used little moves, some push and pull, the direction he faced, and where he was looking to shake up Ranta. Takasagi was trying to knock him back.

There was no doubt about it. Takasagi didn't want to lock blades.

Thinking about it, of course he didn't. Takasagi had a larger build than Ranta. He had more arm strength, too, probably. But Takasagi only had one arm. If he tested that strength against Ranta, who was holding his sword in two hands, even Takasagi was going to struggle with that.

Even if Takasagi was a katana master, there was no changing the fact he'd lost his dominant arm. He couldn't use what he didn't have.

It was true, Ranta's ability was far from touching Takasagi's. Because of that, Ranta had overestimated Takasagi. Basically, he'd been spooked.

He couldn't be overconfident, but being overly hesitant was no good, either. If his spirit were a set of scales, he wanted to keep them balanced. That wasn't easy. Even if it was difficult, though, he'd do it.

"Damn...!" Takasagi shouted.

Maybe out of impatience, Takasagi tried to sweep Ranta's right leg with his own. Ranta hadn't only been cautious of the katana but of leg attacks, too, so he thought he could handle it. In that moment, a certain image appeared in his mind, and Ranta's body moved on its own.

Moving his sword in an upwards rolling motion, he slid his blade along the top of Takasagi's katana. At this point, the tip of his sword was in a position where it could stab into Takasagi's face.

Takasagi also rolled his sword, trying to knock Ranta's sword upwards.

Ranta chose not to resist, and after raising his sword, he rolled it downwards. The tip was aimed at the end of Takasagi's nose again.

Takasagi's one eye went wide.

Ranta pushed the sword in.

Takasagi twisted his body and, gasping, he jumped back.

It was shallow. Too shallow. Ranta's sword had only left a gash about two centimeters long on Takasagi's right cheek. It was just a flesh wound, too.

Ranta retreated with Exhaust, then took a breath. Time to refocus. He had to move on to the next thing.

But, still...

I did it, partner.

He wanted to yell out his name in thanks, but he kept it to himself.

Now isn't the time for getting sentimental. Right, partner?

"That's Wind, huh?" Takasagi lightly spun his left shoulder in a circle, then spat on the ground. His eyes were upturned. They were glazed over. He was different from before, somehow. Wild, yet terribly cold. That was... Bloodlust, huh?

"What, you're a warrior?" Takasagi sneered. "You're not a dread knight?"

Ranta didn't answer. This was the middle of a serious battle. Like he was going to run his mouth. Though, even if he'd wanted to talk, he wasn't sure he could. It was like he'd swallowed a rock or something, because his voice wouldn't come out.

Takasagi.

"You're more skilled than I'd have expected, Ranta. If I trained you for a number of years, I'm sure you'd be pretty useful."

Old man.

Damn, you're scary.

If I take my eyes off you for a second...no, if I take so much as a breath, I might get cut down. That's can't be right, though. I think that, at least, but is that true? Can I say for sure I won't get cut down? I dunno. I can't say for sure. Regardless, this is a completely different Takasagi from before.

A manslayer, that was the word that passed through Ranta's head. Was that Takasagi's true nature?

"For my part, that's what I intended to do," said Takasagi. "For better and for worse, in our group, we're all a bit irresponsible. Between us, that sort of master and student relationship is fundamentally impossible. I thought I was fine with that, but I'm getting on in years. I was stupidly thinking I might try training someone. You had a decent amount of experience, and you'd seen hell. You had guts, too. That tends to be more important than talent. I mean, if you leave a genius alone, they'll grow without you. You're mediocre, but not bad material to work with. I was thinking I'd beat everything I have into you. That it'd be a good way to kill time. I'm disappointed."

Ranta shook his head.

Don't waver.

No matter what Takasagi says, I can't let it bother me. Ignore him. Don't listen.

Besides, why am I letting the old man ramble on like this? He's wasting his breath. There has to be an opening I can take advantage of. There can't be nothing. But despite that...

Not only could Ranta not move forward, but the hand holding his sword was also quivering slightly.

Hey, Zodie. Do something. No dice, huh?

Zodie, who had been pushed down before, had long since gotten up. The demon could hit Takasagi with its naginata from where it was now, but it wasn't budging.

What am I, a frog freezing because a snake's glaring at it?

No—I'm not a frog. I'll eat the damn snake. Eat it whole.

He went to jump, but Takasagi forestalled him. He couldn't imagine that was a coincidence. The timing made it seem like he'd seen right through him.

The next thing he knew, Takasagi was in front of his eyes.

He's huge.

The old man with his one eye opened wide and his lips twisted in a slight smile looked like a giant. Ranta tried to defend himself with RIPer. Though, not intentionally. It was some sort of instinctive self-defense.

Even so, Ranta's sword caught Takasagi's katana. Or perhaps Takasagi had deliberately hit Ranta's sword. He clobbered it, you could say. Or even, he beat the hell out of it.

There was an incredibly loud *clang, clang, clang* sound. Takasagi's katana was like one of the giant's pillars. Ranta's sword was screaming. Ranta was close to screaming himself, too. The one thing he didn't do was close his eyes. That was the best he could manage.

Look, he told himself. *Keep looking. If I don't keep my eyes open and look, I'm dead. He'll kill me. Though, even if I am looking, he may still kill me.*

"Mwahahahahaha…!" Takasagi laughed.

What's with this horrifying creature? Is this guy human? He's a monster.

Ranta didn't think that so much as sensed it. The guy had been released from the limitations of being human. This was crazy. This was clearly impossible.

It wasn't about winning or losing. That wasn't the problem. He was a step away from his will breaking.

But I'm still alive, aren't I?

Even now, he remembered it. It was burned into his memory, and it would never fade.

Deadhead Watching Keep. The keeper orc. The venomously deep red suit of armor and helmet that covered his massive body. The black and gold hair that spilled from his helmet. The two terrifying scimitars. The dual-wielder, Zoran Zesh.

Even Renji had been sent flying, but his partner hadn't flinched. He'd tried to hit him with a Thanks Slash.

Zoran hadn't been just huge; he was fast. He'd hit Ranta's partner before he could get hit. First in the left shoulder. Then the upper right arm. Left forearm. Right hip. Left side of the head. He hit the top of his head, too.

Even after that beating, his partner had still been standing, with Zoran clearly disturbed.

Why won't this human go down? He must have been mystified, and disturbed, too.

It was thanks to Ranta's partner that they'd been able to take Zoran down. Because, until his strength had run out—no, even after that—his partner had stayed on his feet.

Moguzo.

I don't need to shout out that it's thanks to you I'm able to hang in here. I'll risk my life and prove it.

If I do, it'll be the proof that you lived.

It was less that he failed to block the katana, and more that he couldn't block anymore. RIPer was chipped like crazy and went flying. However, that was also his last chance.

When the sword left Ranta's hand, Takasagi swung back as if to kill him with the next blow, and in that instant—

"Ramen...!"

Why did that word come out? Naturally, it was connected to Moguzo & Ranta's Ramen Shop, which he would one day open. In other words, it was hope, it was greed, and it was an expression of his will to live no matter what.

Ranta jumped back with the best Exhaust he could manage.

Naturally, Takasagi chased close behind him. For a middle-aged guy, he was fast!

What are you, old man, a wild beast? Well, I anticipated this, though.

"Keeeeeeeeeeeeeeeeeeeeeeeeeeeeeeeec...!"

Zodie attacked Takasagi from behind. The demon had Takasagi in range of its long naginata all along. The demon had been unable to move because Ranta was intimidated, but once it could move, it was able to attack right away.

Takasagi had to respond. If he didn't, he'd be cut down by the long naginata.

In the end, Takasagi dodged and avoided Zodie's long naginata. Without missing a beat, he yelled, "Oorah...!" and made an incredible thrust that made his arm seem to extend. Not missing its mark, the katana pierced Zodie's chest.

"He..." Zodie turned into something like black steam, and diffused in an instant.

"Rantaaa!" Takasagi turned and shouted.

He couldn't see his face anymore. Or rather, Ranta wasn't looking at Takasagi.

He ran.

He was intent on running.

He didn't think, *I'm not gonna die,* or, *I want to live,* or, *I'm gonna live,* or anything like that. Body and soul, he was running. That was all he was focused on.

The direction didn't matter. He wasn't even consciously fleeing. Ranta just ran and ran.

He kept running with everything he had.

Grimgar of Fantasy and Ash

5 | Unable to Return

THE BUILDINGS in the village were spared from the fire spreading, and most were not burned. It was probably because, if only for a short time, it rained hard.

Fortunately—if anything about this could be said to be fortunate,—the building that she was in was intact, too.

There she was, in the dirt-floored corridor of the building used as a jail. She lay on her back, facing up, with her half-clenched right hand lying by her hip. Her left arm was bent outwards a little, and the palm of her left hand was facing down. Her right leg was bent inwards a little, while her left leg was stretched out almost completely straight.

In no way did it look like she was sleeping. She was hurt badly.

Her face, with its eyelids closed, seemed completely drained of blood.

He wanted to put her limbs in the right position, at least. But what was right? Haruhiro's ability to believe anything was right had long since vanished. He felt like there was nothing just in this world. Everything was wrong, and that was why things had turned out like this.

If you thought about it, that was how it was. It had to be.

Yume walked to her side, furrowed her brow, alternated between pursing and biting her lips, and for a while, she stared down at her. Then she collapsed into a sitting position. Shihoru silently hugged Yume's shoulders.

Kuzaku made no attempt to enter the building.

"...Why?" and "This can't be real..." he was mumbling to himself.

Setora and Kiichi the gray nyaa were outside, too.

Jessie leaned over her...her lifeless head, stroking the stubble on his chin.

As he stood there, Haruhiro's shadow fell on her.

Jessie had called the shaman, or whatever he was, over, and had the man treat Haruhiro, Kuzaku, and Yume.

The shaman was a man with skin like old, cracked leather who resembled neither an orc nor a human, and Jessie addressed him as Niva.

Haruhiro had expected Niva would come with them to the jail, but Jessie hadn't asked him to do that. Haruhiro wasn't all that surprised. Be they a shaman, a priest, or anything else, once a person had lost their one and only life, there was no saving them.

There is a way. Just one, Jessie had said.

Haruhiro hadn't believed those words. There was nothing he could believe. He had no intention of clinging to anything, but still he had brought Jessie to the place where she slept and would not wake.

"I see. Yeah, she's pretty dead." Jessie stated the obvious in blunt terms. Raising his face, he looked at Haruhiro. "May I touch her?"

"You can't," Yume replied instantly. It was a low, slightly hoarse voice, with an awful lot of intensity given it was coming from her. "What're you sayin'? Merry-chan's Yume's comrade. Don't you go touchin' her."

Jessie shrugged. "I thought it would be bad to just touch her, so I'm asking permission."

"Yume's sayin' you can't!"

"Yume." Shihoru hugged Yume close, and glared at Jessie. "...What for? What are you trying to do?"

"I want to check how fresh she is," Jessie said, then smiled wryly. "Ah. That was a poor choice of words. Too blunt? My apologies. *Roundabout...*" He paused as he searched for the appropriate word in the language they all spoke, and said at last, "I'm not so good at saying things in an indirect manner. Basically, if the corpse is too badly damaged, it will cause problems. There's some preparation involved, you see. I want to verify things."

"What... Just what are you preparing to do...?" Shihoru managed.

"Did I not say? There's no question she's dead, but there's one way to resurrect her. I'm preparing to do that, of course."

"Re—" Yume opened her eyes wide, looking from Merry's face to Jessie's and back. "Resurrect... Resurrect? You mean bringin' Merry-chan back to life?"

Jessie didn't respond to Yume's question, turning his gaze instead to Haruhiro. "Can I touch her?"

Haruhiro looked at Shihoru to see her reaction. No, he was looking for help. He couldn't decide anything himself. He could make no decision. If Shihoru didn't nod, Haruhiro would probably keep quiet forever.

Without waiting for Haruhiro's response, Jessie pressed his fingers to Merry's neck, lifted her arm up, and tried bending her fingers. It was like he thought Merry was some kind of doll, and he was testing the range of motion of her joints, and their durability.

Haruhiro felt dizzy. *Stop,* he thought. He wanted to shout at Jessie and kick him away. Why didn't he do it? Probably because he didn't think he had the right.

"She's not in bad shape." Jessie moved his hands away from Merry's body. "If we start right away, there's no real preparation needed. Now it's just a question of what to do."

"...What do you mean, what to do?" Finally opening his mouth, that was all Haruhiro could say.

"Do we resurrect her, or not?" Jessie stood up, then took a short breath. "I can't decide that, after all. It's up to all of you."

"Up to...us?"

"Before that, I guess I should explain at least a little."

"Is there some sort of...condition?" Shihoru asked hesitantly.

"I guess you could call it that." Jessie raised one eyebrow and snorted. "You want to know in advance what will happen, right?"

Had he been listening from outside? Kuzaku came inside the building and knelt next to Haruhiro. Why was he kneeling formally? His big body was twitching.

"Wh...what's going to happen?" Kuzaku asked. "To Merry-san?"

"Well, if I do a certain thing, for the time being, she will come back to life."

Haruhiro tried to say something in response, but his voice failed him.

Hold on.

Wait.

Just wait.

What does that mean, for the time being?

"For the time being." Those are some awfully foreboding words. "For the time being." My chest is so tight, it hurts. The inside of my head is a mess.

"Is there some sort of risk?"

Shihoru was the one to ask the right question. Most likely, the only one with a level head—or the only one trying to keep a level head—was Shihoru.

"'Risk.'" Jessie parroted the word back, cocking his head to the side slightly. "Risk, huh? You could say that, I guess. Let me tell you this, at least. I died once, too, and I came back. I'm not the only one who's come back this way, either. The chance of failure is—well, I won't say it's nonexistent, but you can assume it practically is."

"You..." Kuzaku looked up at Jessie, unable to even speak properly. "You...died once...? Huh...? Died...? Then came ba—Wha?"

"To put it simply, she can come back to life, like me, who already died once. There's no risk, but there is a price to pay. That's because she'll be coming back in my place."

It was hard to understand so suddenly. What had Jessie said?

"She'll be coming back *in my place?*"

"In my place"—What exactly did that mean?

Merry was dead. But he said she could be revived in a certain way. So?

What about Jessie?

"In order to bring Merry back..." Haruhiro's voice sounded like it was echoing somewhere very distant. "...you have to die...?"

"*Yes.* That would be the phenomenon." Jessie said like it was nothing.

"That's..." Shihoru hung her head. "B-but..."

Yume gently hit Shihoru on the back, as if patting her. It was probably an unconscious movement. While Yume's hand moved, she seemed to be thinking.

"Ha ha..." Kuzaku let out a short laugh. He had no idea what was going on anymore, and that may have caused him to laugh despite himself.

"By the way, you people don't need to worry about that part." Jessie's tone was nothing if not disinterested. This clearly involved him, but it was like he didn't feel it had anything to do with him at all. "It was a little scary the first time, but I've experienced it before, so I know what will happen. My Jessie Land's taken a pretty decisive blow. It's too much of a hassle to start over from stage one. I'm happy to call this game over."

"G-game over? That's..." Kuzaku lifted his hips, adjusted his sitting position, and pressed his hands down on his knees. "... Irresponsible, wouldn't you say? Yanni-san is still..."

Jessie sighed and snapped his fingers. "This was never a charity to begin with. I did it because it was fun. If it's gotten boring, then it's over. That's what a game over is, right?"

This man was bizarre.

He'd died once, so since this was his second time—

No, so what if he knows what death is like? He'll still be dying.

No, that's not it, right?

Jessie died once, and, if they took his story at face value, someone had died to bring him back.

Before then, Jessie hadn't been the sort of creature that it was hard to call human, one that could take a Backstab and shrug it off. Jessie had been human. When he came back, that changed.

Haruhiro pressed both his hands on the back of his head. He clutched his hair. By dying and coming back, Jessie ended up like he was now...?

"She can come back to life, like me who already died once," Jessie had said, right?

Didn't that mean... *Merry would end up like Jessie?*

Haruhiro looked at Merry's face. Her smile on the verge of death had vanished. When he inspected her closely like this, honestly, it could only be called a lifeless expression. In fact, she had no expression at all. Because her vital functions had ceased.

He didn't want to recognize it, but the Merry there was nothing more than an object. He couldn't think of her that way, and he couldn't possibly treat her like a thing, but that was the fact. The Merry there was no more than the remains of what had been Merry.

If he didn't use the method Jessie was talking about, Merry wouldn't just stay that way; she wouldn't even be able to maintain the form that was Merry.

Consider the season. She'd start to rot in no time. Eventually the curse of No-Life King would come into effect, and she would start to move.

They had to bury her quickly. Taking the curse into consideration, cremating her would be best. This wasn't Alterna, so there was no crematorium. They'd have to burn her themselves. They would see Merry burning up with their own eyes.

He didn't want to see that. But he probably had no choice. If he didn't see this through, he was sure he'd have regrets. Even if he saw it through, he'd probably have regrets. If it was going to be the same either way, then he should see it. Haruhiro would probably watch.

I don't want to see it.

Even imagining it—no, even attempting to imagine it—every cell in his body felt like it would be crushed to powder. If someone were to ram a hot iron rod into his brain and jerk it around, it might feel like this.

I don't want this.

Merry.

I really don't.

He didn't want to burn her at all. But he had to. The only other option was—

Bringing her back to life.

Jessie was saying it was possible. He would die, and Merry would come back in his place. Was that really a thing that could be done?

If she were his mother, his lover, or someone he had a great debt to, maybe it would be understandable. But that wasn't the case. There was no good reason for him to offer, but Jessie had said he was fine with dying to bring Merry back.

Was there something he wasn't telling them?

For instance, was Jessie thinking he was ready to die, or would rather be dead, and just wanted to die already? Like there was some sort of downside to coming back to life, and though Jessie looked healthy, he actually wasn't? Maybe Jessie felt some sort of suffering or discomfiture, and he was trying to push that off on Merry?

If she came back, what would happen to Merry?

Naturally, Haruhiro wanted her to come back. If it meant a living Merry would come back to him, he'd do anything. He'd be fine with dying himself. In fact, he was ready to offer up his life instead of Jessie's.

But what if that was a result the revived Merry couldn't be happy with? *If it was going to be like this, I wish you'd left me dead.* What if Merry got turned into something that made her feel that way?

"Now then..." Jessie spread his arms wide, and looked around at Haruhiro and each of his comrades.

Haruhiro was suddenly suspicious. What had this man been like before dying? He might have been an entirely different person before then. He might have ended up like this because he was revived. Merry would be the same. If she came back to life, wouldn't this happen to her...?

"What will you do?" Jessie asked. "Bury her, or bring her back? Decide as soon as you can. It'll be a pain to do it if her condition gets worse, and the way things are going, the vooloos will come by sundown. It takes some time, after all. If we're doing it, I want to be done before then."

"...Vooloos?" Shihoru asked in a whisper.

Vooloos. That was a word they weren't hearing for the first time. If he recalled, Jessie and Yanni had been saying it.

He hadn't known what it meant, but, *Vooloo yakah,* he'd said.

It wasn't Jessie, but Setora who was standing by the entrance, who answered. "Vooloos are carrion scavenger wolves."

Her tone was strangely flat.

"They're related to canines, apparently, but they are also cat-like. While they prefer carrion, they will at times attack living creatures—humans and orcs included. They often target hunters who have made a kill and are in the process of carrying it home. The hunter becomes the hunted, and both they and their prey are eaten by the vooloos. With this many dead people lying around, I wouldn't be surprised if the vooloos sniff them out."

"The ones in Thousand Valley are small, right?" Jessie pointed to the north. "East of the Kuaron Mountains, there are vooloos that are bigger than the mist panthers in Thousand Valley. They're the size of bears. If everything had burned, I don't know how things would have been, but it rained. The eagles and crows are probably gathering as we speak. The vooloos will come next. We can chase off eagles and crows, but vooloos are a lot harder. Regardless, we need to abandon this place for now. I've already told Yanni that."

"They've started evacuating?" Shihoru asked.

Jessie responded, "Yes, that is so," with what was probably a deliberately foreign sounding accent. "If they come back here to rebuild, or if they search for another place, that's up to Yanni and the others. I won't get involved. I've lost interest, you see. I don't do things I don't want to do. I decided that before I died, and I've stuck to it."

Jessie paused.

Then he added, "By the way. Since this probably has you worried, just let me say, nothing changed dramatically inside me when I came back to life. That's up to you to believe or not. But I've always had this kind of personality. It did get harder for me to die once I came back, though. That was, well, I guess that's a big change, not a small one. But it wasn't a bad thing. If anything, it's convenient."

"...Details," Haruhiro said, then pressed on his throat.

My voice, it's all hoarse. But yeah. That was it. That's what I wanted to say. Why couldn't I say it before now?

"Please give us details. In concrete terms...if she comes back, how is she going to end up? What happens, and how... Basically, I want to know everything. In order to make a decision. I mean, without really understanding...I can't decide that. Because...it's not about me. I dunno how to say it, but without being able to receive her consent...I'd just be reviving her without permission. I need to think over it carefully. I need material to think on. Without that, while it's not impossible..."

"I refuse to explain."

"Huh?"

Jessie shrugged. "I've told you more or less all I can. There are things I can't tell you myself, you see. You people aren't stupid, so you understand, right? This isn't normal. It's common sense that people can't come back to life, and that's a fact. Things like this almost never happen. This is a special occurrence, and there are unique conditions. It's no miracle, though. Like with a magician's tricks, no matter how mysterious they seem, there's a proper explanation behind it. I can't spoil the trick. I have a reason why. I can't tell you that reason, either. What will you do? Accept my offer, and bring her back to life? Or will you bury her? Decide already. I don't care which it is."

Haruhiro gazed up to the heavens.

There was a hole. He could see the sky. Whether the sky was clear and blue, or black with thick clouds, what difference did it make?

That didn't just go for the sky. For now, at least, he probably had no interest in anything. For now. Was it only now? Tomorrow, the next day, and beyond—as time passed, would that change?

Yeah, that was a thing that happened, huh? This happened, too. She was alive, huh? We spent time together, huh?

Would he be able to look back and remember it like that?

"Please," Haruhiro said, his gaze still fixed on the sky he could see through the hole in the ceiling. "If you can really do it, I want you to bring Merry back."

Is this a bad dream, or a scam? He still couldn't shake those doubts. *The next moment, I'll wake up, Merry and I will be alone together, and Merry will be dead. There's no one else around. There's nothing I can do. Merry is just dead.*

Or Jessie will say, "Sorry," with a half-hearted laugh. "It was all a lie. My bad. Was just pulling your leg a bit. You know there's no way to bring back the dead, right?"

It was neither.

"Well, let's get to work, then."

What would they do? What was about to start?

Bizarrely, it wasn't just Haruhiro, Yume, Kuzaku, or Setora who was still by the door who said nothing. Even Shihoru didn't ask Jessie about it.

No one opened their mouth, but when Jessie said, "Could you move? You're in the way," Yume and Shihoru backed away without a word, as did Kuzaku and Haruhiro.

Jessie pulled out a knife, pressing it to his own wrist. Then, he said, "If Yanni or the others come, do not, under any circumstances, let them in. This is going to take hours. I won't tell you not to watch, but there's no need to watch the whole thing. Some of you go outside and stand guard."

First Kuzaku, and then Yume, stumbled out on unsteady legs. Yume was in a daze, and Kuzaku was tearing up.

Shihoru remained. Haruhiro stayed, too.

Jessie knelt next to Merry and mumbled, "It's here, right?" He slit his left wrist. He showed no sign of hesitation. It looked like he'd cut fairly deep, because the blood didn't just flow, it gushed out. Jessie said, "Oops," and hurriedly pressed the cut against Merry's shoulder.

There was a horrifying wound there. That was where she had been bitten by the guorella, and that wound may have been the direct cause of Merry's death. It was clear that Jessie was trying to touch the cut he had just made in his wrist to Merry's wound. What good would that do? Haruhiro had no idea. It was a horrific sight, but Haruhiro didn't stop him.

Jessie discarded the knife, clutching his left wrist with his right hand. He seemed to be trying to fix it in place. He took a breath. He grimaced.

"Haruhiro," he called.

"...Ah..." Haruhiro had meant to reply, but his voice hardly came out.

"Could you help me a bit here?"

"...With what?"

"I'm holding it in place, but I want to keep it from separating better. This is my first time doing this, so I don't really know the process that well. I think it'll be fine, though. You know what they say, proceed with due caution, right?"

It was Shihoru who did as he asked. She found a large piece

of cloth in her belongings and, with her whole body trembling, and sharp labored breaths, she wrapped it around Jessie's left wrist and Merry's neck.

Haruhiro did nothing. He couldn't do a thing. He just watched.

Shihoru returned, wiping her hands on the hem of her robe.

"...Sorry," Haruhiro apologized in a small voice.

Shihoru wrapped both her arms around Haruhiro's right arm and turned her head to the side. She was still trembling. It must have been hard enough just standing. Shihoru wanted his support.

Even I can manage that much, so I have to do it, and I ought to, Haruhiro thought.

"Haruhiro-kun, if you hadn't said it..." she said softly.

I was wrong.

That wasn't it.

"...I would have," she finished. "'Revive Merry'...I'd have said... so don't shoulder this by yourself. Because Yume and Kuzaku-kun...I'm sure they'd have done the same."

"Yeah." Haruhiro nodded.

Shihoru hadn't wanted him to support her. She had been trying to support Haruhiro herself.

The one who was about to collapse right now...was Haruhiro.

"I..."

While he was unable to get another word out, Shihoru held Haruhiro's hand tight.

He'd sworn, if nothing else, he'd have no regrets. He didn't know what Merry would think, and he might cause her suffering. Even so, Haruhiro could not let himself regret this. If this decision was wrong, and he'd made a mistake, Haruhiro would take the blame. He couldn't complain if Merry resented him. Let her. But he'd had no other choice.

Taking any other option just wasn't possible for him. No matter how many times he went over that scene, Haruhiro would ultimately have always asked Jessie to do it. He might not even have wavered over it.

If Merry could come back to life, of course he would wish for that. So he would have no regrets.

Haruhiro squeezed Shihoru's hand in return. His heart was no longer racing. He didn't have trouble breathing, either.

There was a lot of noise outside for some reason.

Caw. Caw. Caw. Caw, ca-caw. Caw. Caw. Caw.

Was that sound of birds? He looked to the hole in the ceiling. There were many black points flying back and forth in the sky. It looked like it really was birds.

Jessie had been kneeling with his right knee down and his left knee up. Now both knees were down. His shoulders were moving up and down slightly. He'd started coughing, too.

Haruhiro perked up his ears, but Jessie's voice was so quiet, he couldn't make it out. However, rather than talking to himself, Jessie seemed to be talking to someone else.

Who exactly? Merry? But Jessie wasn't looking at Merry's face. His eyes were on the ground.

"Damn...!" Kuzaku yelled outside.

When Haruhiro looked, the birds had gathered and de-scended. The fairly large birds were eagles, and the comparatively smaller ones were crows, apparently. The birds were swarming around the corpses that had once been the gumow residents of Jessie Land, and around the guorellas.

Kuzaku swung his large katana around, trying to drive the birds off, but there were just too many of them. Yume was occasionally swinging her katana, but only to menace any birds that came near her.

He didn't see Setora and Kiichi. Had they gone off some-where?

"Shihoru," Haruhiro said.

"...Hm? What?"

"Why don't you sit?"

"I'm...fine."

"I see."

"What about you, Haruhiro-kun? Are you okay?"

He came close to saying, *I don't know,* but swallowed the words.

"I'm fine. Me, too."

"...Okay."

"Yeah."

Jessie didn't just have two knees on the ground; his right el-bow was on the ground now, too.

That man doesn't look fine at all, Haruhiro thought, but he couldn't get into the mood to say anything to him.

Merry would come back to life in Jessie's place.

What exactly does that mean? he came close to wondering again. Haruhiro shook his head. *Let's not do this. Even if I think about it, nothing will change. Besides which, it's too late. No, he's not done yet, so it might not be too late to act. Still, I have no intention of stopping Jessie now. Whatever else happens, Merry will return to life. I can see Merry again. Isn't that good enough? It might not be good, but that's fine.*

Crows landed on the hole in the ceiling and started cawing. It was noisy, so he wanted to chase them off, but it was higher than he could reach by jumping and swinging his stiletto. Should he ask Shihoru to do it? With Dark? There was no need to go that far. For now, they showed no sign of coming in through the hole, so he could leave them be.

Jessie finally had his forehead on the ground. Haruhiro couldn't hear him talking anymore. His back was moving slowly, and slightly. He was apparently not dead.

But it was bizarre. Even after being hit by Backstab, Jessie had been fine. He hadn't treated it, but the wound had healed on its own. And what about the wound from before?

That time, Haruhiro's stiletto had definitely punctured his kidney. It had been a fatal wound. It'd healed, but now the man was in this bad shape from a mere cut to his arm?

It was weird.

Caw, caw, caw. Caw, caw, caw. Caw, caw, caw, caw.

The crows were cawing. There were a lot more of them than before. Not just four or five. There were easily more than ten.

"Sma...ller...?" Shihoru said.

He got a chill.

Was it a trick his eyes were playing on him? Was he just imagining it?

Jessie hadn't been a mass of muscle to begin with, and he hadn't been exceptionally tall, either. Even so, the size of his body... Was it because he was crouching? It was hard to imagine that was it. He was clearly smaller. Jessie had gotten smaller. There was less of him, you could say.

Haruhiro squinted. *It's no good,* he thought. *I can't see well enough from here.*

Shihoru let go of his arm.

Haruhiro moved to a spot where he could see the profile of Jessie's face. He used Sneaking, not consciously, just naturally.

Jessie's cheeks and eyes were extremely sunken, and he looked emaciated. Or perhaps "desiccated" was the better word. It wasn't just his face. His whole body had lost its thickness. His collapsed torso, his bent legs,...they were unpleasantly thin. Jessie's arms had never been that thin before. They were like twigs now.

Caw, caw, caw.

Caw, caw, caw.

Caw, caw, caw, caw, caw.

The crows were cawing noisily.

Jessie shrank more and more.

What was this?

Why had he not found it strange sooner?

Jessie had slit his wrist. Even if the wound healed, he would lose a large amount of blood in a short time. Even if he pressed the opening of the wound against Merry's injury, tying it there with a piece of cloth like that, it would make little difference. The cloth would be soaked in blood in no time, and a sea of blood would spread out. However, that didn't happen.

Jessie kept on shrinking. Like he'd been nothing but a bag of blood. Like the skin on the outside had held the human form of Jessie, and the inside was filled with blood. Like, if the blood was let out, only the skin would remain. But that was impossible, of course. If he hadn't had bones, and muscles, and organs, he couldn't have walked around or breathed.

"...No way." Shihoru covered her mouth.

Jessie was practically flat at this point.

What the hell was this?

Caw, caw, caw, caw, caw, caw, caw, caw, caw, caw, caw, caw.

The crows were cawing shrilly.

Haruhiro threw up. There was no going back. He knew that.

Really? No, that wasn't true. If he acted now, he could still take it back. He honestly thought that might be for the best. However, if he pulled Jessie, who had become like a leather bag now, away from Merry, that possibility would vanish entirely. He would never be able to meet with Merry again.

Was he okay with that?

Grimgar
of
Fantasy and Ash

6 | **Keep Up Appearances**

I'M COUGHING *all of a sudden. Could I be sick? Like, with some-thing really bad? No? Yeah, probably not. It's just a cough. There's no meaning behind it. It's a cough without meaning. A meaningless cough. —Wait, why am I thinking this boring stuff? I'm such a moron.*

Ranta was really bothered for some reason, and he looked left, then right.

He rubbed his eyes. Doing that wouldn't make him see any better, though.

"It's pretty dark..."

Judging by the color of the sky peeking through the trees, the sun still shouldn't have set. Despite that, the deep forest of Thousand Valley was enveloped in fog.

I'm not scared. Well, no. No matter how many nights I spend alone, it's impossible to wipe away the fear and uncertainty. There's no point in acting tough. It's not like anyone is watching. I could put up a strong front, but it wouldn't mean a thing.

"Hehe..." Zodiac-kun the demon let out a slight laugh behind him.

He'd have given the demon a piece of his mind, as he had in the past, but now it didn't even bother him that much. Demons acted like another person with their own personality, but that was by no means what they were. It was said that revelations from Skullhell were reflected in a demon's actions. However, the demon was fundamentally a mirror of their dread knight, an extension of them. Even if a demon looked wildly different from their dread knight, they were merely a surfacing of a hidden facet of their dread knight, or a part of themselves they didn't know.

"Hehehe... Trip... Trip now... Trip and fall right there... Trip and die..."

"Nah, but I don't feel that way about myself, you know?" Ranta said. "There's no way I would, right?"

"..."

"I'm getting the silent treatment, huh?"

"..."

"Just disappear already. Get lost. No, that was a lie. I was lying, okay? Don't you disappear on me, all right?"

"What...should I do...? Hehe..."

"Command: Don't disappear."

"Tsk..."

"What, why the ominous tongue click...?"

Zodiac seemed dissatisfied, but the demon didn't up and disappear.

When a lord in the Alterna dread knights' guild had demonstrated how to control a demon, Ranta faintly remembered them using the word "Command" to make it obey. It seemed to be effective when he tried it, so he had been using it from time to time.

A demon was subservient to their dread knight. If the demon disobeyed, it would be nothing other than proof that the dread knight couldn't control himself. By extension, that would mean he didn't understand himself.

After all, because the demon was himself, it was unthinkable that he would be unable to understand it.

Naturally, Ranta had a full grasp of himself. It was impossible he wouldn't be able to make himself do as he wanted. He felt like he'd long since convinced himself of that, past the point of any doubt. That had to be proof that he hadn't understood himself in the slightest. He hadn't thought deeply about it. Probably, he hadn't wanted to.

I'm me. The me right here is 100% me. Isn't that enough?

But what do I mean, 100%? What do I mean, me? Who the hell do I think I am? Who? There's no way I can answer that. I mean, I don't really get me. I've never been able to see myself.

What was I looking at before now? If I wasn't even able to see myself, then what about others? Like, was I accurately judging Haruhiro and the rest? Didn't I just have a warped perception of them, decided by what was convenient for me?

That'd be part of me, too...is what I guess that means, though. That's the kind of person I am. Self-centered, selfish, and unrepentant. Why am I like this?

In the end, it may be that I don't expect anything from other people. You guys, I'm sure none of you liked me anyway, right? I knew that all along. Like, you'd never like me, would you?

Yume, Shihoru, and Merry hated me. I never once thought they were only pretending to hate me, and maybe they actually did like me.

Kuzaku didn't like me, either. Well, he hated me pretty badly. I put up with that a bit, since he was younger and less experienced, but if not for that, I'd have pushed back harder.

I was only with Manato for a really short time, but I'm still left with the feeling he was doing a good job of handling me. He was a smart man. He probably thought it was a mistake to let his like or dislike of me cloud his judgment, and was used to controlling his emotions. That's the type he was. That was easy on me.

Moguzo was a mystery. No, there was nothing mysterious about him. It's just that he was a rare breed, so I found him mysterious.

He was a nice guy. A really good guy. He put others before himself, never butting in where he didn't belong, and was just trying his hardest. He went a little beyond his limits for his comrades, and he died for it. That fight with Zoran Zesh at Deadhead Watching Keep. If Moguzo hadn't been there, Renji, Kajiko, and the Wild Angels would have been in trouble. At the very least, a number of them would probably have died. Maybe every volunteer soldier there would have been wiped out.

Moguzo must have understood that, so he had to do it. If he hadn't dug in his heels there, everyone would've been dead. He threw his life away for all of us. That was the kind of guy he was.

I don't think Moguzo hated me. I seriously believe that. I did a lot of stuff that it would be no wonder if he'd hated me for, but that guy wouldn't hate the comrades he fought alongside.

Then, there was Haruhiro.

He hated me, obviously. It's no exaggeration to say he detested me for being the troublesome dread knight. He did a good job putting up with me, though. It goes beyond the level where I can be impressed, and instead it's just exasperating. Was he stupid? I mean, seriously, that guy. He has to be a total masochist.

I don't think I went out of my way to make trouble for Haruhiro. That wasn't my intention, but I never tried to make everything easier for him, either. I was always like, "You adapt to me. So that things are easier for me, you sort things out properly, and get a proper environment together. Make it so I can feel good about putting my awesome powers to use. You're the leader, aren't you? If you're the leader, this should be a given. That's what we have a leader for, after all. The ability to adjust? Basically, that's everything."

Well, Parupiro, you know what? I'm sure it's hard on you, too, but them's the breaks, right? It's not like it's easy for me. Your luck ran out when you took on the role of leader. Give it up. Or work hard. It's not my problem. I'm not you. No one else can be me, and no one else can be you. We're all alone after all, right?

Man, some guy I am. For someone who doesn't expect things of other people, I leave things up to them entirely, and then expect them to baby me.

"Not that reflecting on it at this point is gonna do me any good..." he muttered.

"Ehe... Hehehe... You inferior monkey who can't reflect on your failures... Hehehe..."

Ranta turned back and glared at Zodiac-kun. The demon was wearing that thing again, damn it. It had a purple sheet-like thing over its head. Its two eyes were like holes, and there was a gash-like mouth beneath them. In its right hand it held a knife, and in its left hand a club. Even though the demon was floating, it had two all-too-real legs growing out of it.

"Like, didn't you turn from Zodiac-kun into Zodie...?" Ranta complained.

"Kehe... When you haven't made any offerings...don't get uppity... Be quiet and die forever..."

"Command: Don't tell me to die."

"...Discorporate."

"Synonyms aren't okay either, all right?"

"...Get killed."

"Using a passive is the same thing, dammit ."

"Where did the you who loved freedom pass on to... Ranta...?"

"With freedom comes responsibility. Also, don't subtly work in a reference to me passing away."

"Heh... Heheheh... Responsibility, huh...? That's the word that suits you the least..."

"Even now, when I've ended up like this taking responsibility for my own actions?"

"Do you regret it, Ranta...? How cheeky of you... Hehehe..."

"No. I don't regret it."

"Trying to act tough... Hehehe..."

"I'm seriously not trying to act tough," Ranta shot back. "There are probably a whole bunch of things I'd never've realized if this hadn't happened. I won't go as far as to say this was for the best, but I'm satisfied with it. No matter what happens to me from here on, the one thing I won't do is regret it."

"He..."

"Was I too cool there?"

"...Bleeeeeeeeeeeeeuuuch."

"You're puking?!"

That was his demon, all right. It never forgot its sense of humor. A sense of humor was essential for any man. With humor came composure. Women were drawn to men who were composed over men who were on edge. Not that there are any women around, though.

Should he rest? Or keep going?

He questioned that every few dozen minutes. Few dozen minutes? Was it more frequent? Maybe it was every few minutes. He couldn't track the time, so he didn't know.

When night approached, the forest got loud. It hadn't exactly been quiet during the day, but the noisiness at night was different. He couldn't see in the dark, so his sense of hearing was likely heightened. He became sensitive to every noise. He was almost wholly reliant on sounds.

"Maybe we shouldn't talk," Ranta said in an undertone. "Hey, Zodiac-kun. Command: Shut up unless you sense something really bad coming."

Once he made Zodiac-kun shut its mouth, the unceasing sounds of the forest pressed in on his ears even more.

Sounds. Sounds. He couldn't let himself be batted around by the onrushing sounds.

Listen, and sort them out, he told himself. *It's extremely hard to, but I have to do it. What am I hearing close by? My own footsteps. The chirping of insects. That's about it, huh? What is that high-pitched "fii, fii, fii, fii" I'm hearing the cry of? I dunno. How about that "cah, cah, cah, cacacacacacah" noise? How should I know? I'm no professor of nighttime forests.*

This pisses me off. Sure, I'm a dread knight, not a professor of nighttime forests. Besides, what's a professor of nighttime forests, anyway? No, but still, if it's necessary, I'll become a professor of nighttime forests, or whatever I have to be. I have to. Or maybe I don't? I dunno.

Is it reckless pressing on when it's this dark, after all? I'm at my limit, right? This is clearly dangerous. Maybe I should rest? If I go to sleep, when I wake up, it'll be morning. Well, if something happens while I'm sleeping, I'll cross that bridge when I come to it. The old man has to be sleeping by now, too, right? Is he even after me still? The old man's goal was to bring me back, I mean, and I have no intention of going. In that case, wouldn't he decide he'd had enough and head back? If he has, there's no need to rush. I can take it easy and prioritize safety as I go.

It's no good.

I'm scared.

This is damn scary!

Too damn scary, okay?! My heart's racing like crazy! I've never been this scared before! Why?!

"...Oh."

Up until now, he had been on the run. He was trying not to get caught, of course, and he'd been afraid whenever he sensed a pursuer, but it was Takasagi and his people he had been up against. They wouldn't just up and kill him without talking first. That had been his view, and, as a matter of fact, it turned out he'd been right.

And so, as long as Takasagi and his men were chasing him, Ranta had, in a way, not been alone. At the very least, he hadn't had a sense of how truly, hopelessly alone he was.

In the vastness of Thousand Valley, which was likely filled with dangers, he didn't even know what direction he was heading in.

Besides, where was he headed, and what was he trying to do?

He was sort of thinking, *I guess I'll head back to Alterna.* But he had no precise idea what he'd do when he got there.

If I run into Renji, maybe he'll let me join his party, was one vague thought he had. *I turned him down once. Maybe that's not gonna happen.*

Could he get back? To Alterna?

In this situation, with no basis to think so, he wasn't stupid enough to confidently believe, *Yeah, I'll bet I can.*

This was solitude.

He was truly alone without a friend in the world.

He wanted to rest. In order to recover his stamina, and to keep his risk level to a minimum, it was best if he did. He didn't need to sleep. He just had to lie down, or even sit. He knew that in his head.

But he couldn't rest.

If he stopped, he'd probably go crazy. At the bare minimum, he'd cry. Or rather, Ranta had started to tear up at some point. He was embarrassed by it, but he'd started weeping. No, he didn't have the composure to feel embarrassed.

He could only keep his demon materialized for thirty minutes consecutively. Before he noticed it, Zodiac-kun had vanished, and he wanted to scream.

If you're going away, tell me! Tell me before you disappear!

Through sobs, he hurriedly recast Demon Call. Zodiac-kun did as Ranta had instructed, and the demon continued to avoid unnecessary talk. Ranta had given the order himself, so he couldn't complain. If he rescinded the command, it would be admitting defeat.

No, that wasn't the problem. If he carried on his comedy routine-like banter with Zodiac-kun, well, it would distract him, but in a way it was like he was playing both the joker and the straight man, and that felt empty.

No, no, that wasn't the problem. It was more like... Wait, why had he ordered Zodiac-kun not to talk in the first place? He couldn't quite remember anymore, but a man never went back on his word, and his pride wouldn't allow him to admit he was lonely and to ask Zodiac-kun to let loose with a funny story or two.

That's right. If Zodiac-kun asked me, I'd be willing to oblige, but I can't let myself be the one to bow my head. Besides, my demon is like a part of me, so it's strange to think about who's asking who for things... In other words, can't Zodiac-kun guess at my feelings and hit me with a gag? Well, why not? Huh? How about it? I'm asking a question here. No, I guess I'm not asking, huh? I'm not asking. Even without me asking, you should figure it out. Figure it out, please. Why won't you figure it out? I'm sad. This is tough. Seriously, seriously tough...

It had gotten a bit brighter, and he had a better grasp of the outlines of the trees and terrain. In that one night, he felt like he'd aged twenty, maybe thirty years. That was how thoroughly exhausted he felt.

"I guess that means...I'm safe...?" he murmured.

No. It was too soon to decide that. The night wasn't even over yet.

One more push.

He was almost there.

Almost where? What's going to happen?

Even if the morning did come, there was no guarantee he'd be safe. When was he going to be able to rest?

Anytime. If he was prepared to accept whatever the consequences were, he could rest anywhere and in any way he wanted.

It's just a matter of being prepared to accept it. But that means giving up. No, it means pivoting. I've come this far. I'm at my limit. Keeping my feet moving forward is more pain than I can bear. I never knew a single step could be so taxing. I should rest. If I don't, I'll collapse. I have no other choice.

Make the decision, and let myself rest. I'm sure it'll be fine. The things I'm worried about won't happen. I'll take a quick nap, and when I'm feeling better, I'll be able to move again.

He stopped.

"All right..."

Even his voice was weak.

See? There's no choice but to rest now.

He tried to sit down on the ground.

"Heh... Ranran..."

"...Huh?"

Hearing his name being called, he turned back. *Who're you calling Ranran?* he wanted to say, but now wasn't the time.

Zodiac-kun was trying to do an about-face.

Ranta reacted by quickly using Exhaust. Right afterward, or more like at the exact same time, Zodiac-kun was pinned to the ground by something.

Whatever it was, it had come from close by, leaping out of the bushes behind Ranta and Zodiac-kun to attack the demon. Before Zodiac-kun could fight back, it dug its fangs into the area near the demon's hole-like eyes.

When a demon received a lethal amount of damage, it crumbled away as easily as a sandcastle. When that happened, their assailant might have been surprised by that. But it quickly assumed a low posture and came in Ranta's direction.

What was that thing?

A beast? It's blackish. No, it's spotted. Is it a wolf? No, it's a cat? Is it a leopard or something?

Oh, damn. It's fast.

He had no sword. He'd lost it in the fight with Takasagi. This was beyond bad.

Ranta pulled his spare knife while backing away further with Exhaust, but what was he supposed to do with a weapon like this?

He used Exhaust again.

It's no good. I can't pull away. Not only that, it's getting closer fast. It's on a different level from a human or orc. It's too fast. It's no good. I can't run away.

Ranta was totally losing it. That was probably why.

"Wha...?!"

It was a tree. He slammed his back into a tree. What a blunder.

It was coming. The leopard. It was probably a leopard. It roared and pounced at him.

It pinned him. The pressure was incredible. He was pressed to the ground. He couldn't move his arms.

Ranta was wearing a helmet. Its movable visor flew off. It looked like the leopard had torn it off with its bite.

"Ohhhhhhhhh...?!"

What came next was crazy. It tried to bite his face. Ranta instinctively twisted his neck. The leopard ended up biting his head, not his face.

"Ohhh, ohhhhh, ohhhhhhh...?!"

It was gnawing on it. His helmet. Yes. His helmet. Somehow his helmet was holding back the leopard's fangs.

No...?

"Yowch?!"

It hurts?

It hurts when you do that, okay?

"Ohhhhhhhh, ohhhhhhhhhh, noooooooooooooo...?!"

His helmet. Under the immense power of its fangs. Its fangs had probably punctured the helmet. Those fangs were sinking into Ranta's head. Maybe not that deeply just yet, but it hurt so they were definitely stabbing into him. Also, his helmet seemed ready to crumple, or it already had started to, and his neck felt like it was going to break.

I'm dead. I am so dead here. It's gonna eat me.

"I-I-I-I-I'm not tasty, so h-h-hold on, don't eat me, don't eat me, don't eat me! Don't eat me, wahhhhhhhhhhhhhhhhhh...?!" He was starting to panic.

Calm down, he told himself. *Right now, it's time to take a chill pill. I don't think I could pop a pill now, but it's a figure of speech.*

"Ah! Ahhhh! O Darkness, O Lord of Vice, Dread Terror...!"

A purplish haze arose, and it was sucked into the leopard's nose and mouth.

The effect was instant. The leopard jumped away from Ranta.

Ranta immediately rolled to the side and got on all fours. He jumped with Leap Out.

While fleeing, he turned back to look at the leopard. The leopard let out a cat-like yowl as it jumped around. It was like there was something dreadful in front of it, and it was trying to sweep whatever it was away with its front legs. That was how it looked.

Terrifying the target with menace of the dark god Skullhell, and robbing it of its ability to make proper decisions. Dread Terror was working. It would be perfect if he could run away now, but things probably weren't going to be that easy.

The leopard roared and turned his way. It was coming. In no time, it came after him at top speed.

Could he be heading towards death, maybe?

To use dread magic, he had to stop. If he stopped, it would catch up to him in an instant, and he'd be pushed down. Intercepting it was a no-go. That leopard was bigger than Ranta. He wouldn't stand a chance with this knife.

The leopard probably lacked stamina, so if he could keep running, he could probably aim to tire it out, but it was fast. The leopard was too fast. It would catch him soon. There was only one thing to do.

For the leopard, Ranta was prey. It must have been trying to eat him. It was hungry. It wanted to eat. In that case, he just had to feed it. Yeah. It could have an arm.

All right, I've decided. It's so I can survive. This is a cheap price. No big deal. I'll live. I'm gonna live. Steel myself, keep my head cool, focus on how to survive, and make my choice. I'll damn well do it. I can do this. Believe.

He came to a sudden stop. The leopard was almost upon him. It was right in front of his nose, you could say.

Missing.

He made it look like he'd go right, then went left.

The leopard followed him with almost no confusion. Seriously? Those were some serious natural instincts.

One more time, Missing. This time he feinted right, then went left.

Hold out, legs!

The leopard was shaken to the right a bit, but it still followed him closely.

"Hah...!"

This wasn't Leap Out or Exhaust. Ranta twisted his body as he leapt pretty much straight up. Not high, but low and sharp.

He'd have the onrushing leopard go past him. No, that wasn't it.

He grabbed on to the leopard's back.

He was ready to sacrifice an arm if need be, but he wasn't about to give it up from the get-go.

Ranta wrapped his arm around the leopard's neck, holding onto its torso with both his legs. He stabbed his knife into the side of its neck. He tried to dig in deep, but the leopard yelped and jumped. It slammed, back first, into a nearby tree.

The one who took the direct damage from that was Ranta, who was clinging to its back. The impact. He came close to blacking out.

I won't let go. I'm not going anywhere.

"Unghhhhhhhhhhhhhhhhhhhhhhhhhh...!"

He moved the knife.

Die. Die. Die, damn it.

The leopard flailed around, pawing at Ranta's left arm. Its claws. Their power was incredible.

His left arm was torn loose.

Now was the time—not to be stubborn.

Get away, he thought. He rolled, then got up. The leopard pounced.

He fled with Exhaust and Missing, somehow managing to get away, but the leopard hadn't slowed at all. It was as if that neck wound didn't so much as itch.

Ranta pulled off his crushed helmet, threw it at the leopard, and jumped with Exhaust. This was getting to be pretty taxing on his legs. How far could he go? He'd have to see. Because determination alone wasn't going to be enough.

This was the time to look for a way to turn things around, but he didn't have one. One more time. He'd have to do the same thing again. If it was just once more, he could manage somehow. Once he couldn't move properly, he'd have to make sacrifices.

He wasn't straining himself. It wasn't any sort of pathetic determination, either. This was a clear crisis, a life or death situation, and he was standing on the edge, but he was strangely relaxed.

If he weren't, he'd have been shocked senseless when a long, thin object dropped from above as the leopard was closing in.

Naturally, *Oh,* he was surprised, but he was nicely relaxed, so he was able to react immediately. That long object was stabbed into the ground right in front of Ranta's fingertips. It was a katana.

The instant Ranta cast aside his knife, he pulled the katana from the ground. Pulling the hilt back to his left ear, he held it with both hands. His right foot forward, his left foot in back.

The leopard was close. Too damn close.

He moved his left foot forward, turning his wrist as he swung diagonally down and to the right.

He felt it hit something.

The leopard went past his right side, close enough it may or may not have touched him, and collapsed.

"This katana..." Ranta murmured.

In front of him on the left... It wasn't fit to be called a hill, but there was a sharp swell in the ground there.

Someone had thrown him this katana from up there. He could only imagine that was the case. There was no way something so convenient would just rain down from the sky, so he could say the chances of it being anything else were nil.

He knew it would be pointless, but Ranta clambered up the slope.

It wasn't pointless. There was no one there, but there was a discarded katana sheathe.

Ranta crouched and reached for the sheathe. He grasped it, and his knees gave out.

He let out a silent sob.

Don't cry.

I can't shed tears.

Hold it in with everything I've got, and breathe.

"That old man..."

He tried to laugh, but it didn't work.

"What an idiot..."

Grimgar
of
Fantasy and Ash

7 | **Guidepost**

I RUN.
Run.
It's dark.
I run down a long, pitch-black tunnel.
I can see what looks like light up ahead.
I head for it, and run.
Run.

Run.

I run through the dark.
Towards the light, I run.
I can't seem to reach it. Even so, I run.
Run.

Run.

Almost there. Just a little further.

It feels like the tunnel is about to end, but it never does.

I run.

Run.

Run.

I keep running, and...

Suddenly, the light overflows.

Leaving the tunnel, I run.

Run.

Run as far as I can.

In the sunlight, my exposed arms and head feel hot.

When I run, it feels nice and cool, so I don't want to stop.

I run.

Run through the grass.

When I turn back, the sun gets in my eyes, and it's blinding.

That seems funny to me somehow, and I laugh.

As I laugh, I turn back to the front, and run.

"Hey, don't go too far."

I hear a voice saying that.

"Nah," I reply, laugh again, and pick up my pace.

I don't want to get caught, I think.

I don't want to be caught by anybody.

Not that there's anywhere I want to go.

Even without the wind, when I run like this, it feels like the wind is blowing.

...Hey, seriously... Come back already.

I hear the voice again.

I guess I have to, I think, and stop.

Dad is always busy with work, and he doesn't get enough exercise. He loves recording everything with his video camera, so he takes his daughter out on his day off, and we drive to somewhere a little way off, though sometimes we just walk to the nearby park, too, but, anyway, he takes me somewhere and rolls the camera. He did at my preschool graduation and school entrance ceremony. Hina-matsuri and Christmas. Also, my birthdays.

But for all that he records, he hardly ever watches it, right?

"That's fine," my dad says. "It's a record. Someday, there will be a time when we really want to watch it. We can all watch together and reminisce. I'm recording for when that time comes."

"Like, when I grow up?" I ask.

"Well, for one example," Dad answers, "when you grow up, get married, and have a child of your own..."

It feels very strange to hear that. Me, get married?

"You can't say for sure you won't, right? Well, it would be completely unsurprising if you did. Probably, someday, you'll get married to someone, I think."

...Will I? Get married? Have children? Does that mean I'll become a mother?

"You might become one," Dad says.

I have the feeling that won't happen.

"...Huh? What? Say that again," I murmured. "Hold on... I couldn't hear you that well."

Mom is saying something over the phone. Mom is crying. I can't hear her well through her tears.

But, honestly, I understand. I heard her say Dad died just fine.

But I think it must be a lie, or I must have misheard. I mean, it feels like something that could never happen, so I ask her to repeat it.

Huh?

What, Mom? Speak properly.

What happened to Dad...?

Run.

I run.

I run through the hall at school.

Out the door, I run.

Coming to a major street, as I run, I search for a taxi. I raise my hand, and run.

I jump into the cab that stops for me. I tell the driver my destination. The taxi crawls along. When a light turns red, it stops.

This is so, so slow, I think. *If it was going to be like this, I shouldn't have taken a cab. I should have run.*

The taxi stops in front of the hospital. I try to get out. The door won't open.

"Miss, the fare. You have to pay your fare," I'm told.

"How much?" I ask, pulling out my wallet.

I go pale.

Inside it, there's only 425 yen. Not enough.

What'll I do, what'll I do?

"Um, my dad died, so, I'm sorry, about the money..." I stammer.

"Oh, it's fine, it's fine, I get it." The driver opens the door.

"I'm sorry, I'm sorry, I'm sorry," I apologize repeatedly, get out of the cab, and I run. I run around inside the hospital.

In a dark place, I watch the videos Dad took. I'm running. Laughing. Acting polite. Blowing out candles on a cake. Singing.

Sometimes, I hear Dad's voice. Like, "Hey, don't go too far."

There's Dad's laughter.

When I sing, Dad sings, too.

I sit on the floor in a room with the lights out, watching the images of myself on the television for who knows how long.

Dad's face never appears once. Not even his hands do.

I only hear his voice. But, occasionally, I think.

Why didn't I record Dad, too?

"Please, go out with me," Hakamada-kun says to me beneath a tree. I think about it. Then, I respond.

"What exactly does that involve?" I asked.

"...What does it involve? Like...going home together and stuff?"

"I just have to walk home with you?"

"No, not just that...like, going out to play, too?"

"I don't mind playing, but..."

"But what?"

"It's fine, really."

I guess we'll end up getting married, I'm thinking.

Hakamada-kun isn't saying anything about marriage, of course. He hasn't said a word about it.

But what does it mean to go out when you aren't considering getting married? I end up wondering.

"What's so great about Hakamada?" Yakki asks me, and I tilt my head to the side in thought.

Yakki has her bike parked next to the bench, and she's eating an ice pop. I'm eating one myself, too. The summer cicadas are noisy, and my ice pop is super cold, but I'm not sweating.

"Nothing's all that great about him," I answer honestly.

"He's no good at all, but you're still going out with him?" Yakki asks me.

"We say we're going out, but about all we really do is walk home together."

"That's what we call going out," Yakki said. "Well, did you two kiss, at least?"

"That hasn't happened."

"What, you don't wanna?"

"I've never once thought I wanted to, I guess."

"Why are you even going out with him?"

Well, if I have to say something, maybe I felt like going out with someone wouldn't be so bad, but now that I think about it, I feel like it's a little different from that.

While I'm unable to give an answer, Yakki suggests, "Maybe you should call it off?"

I think so, too. But how should I tell that to Hakamada-kun?

When I take my slippers out of my locker and put them on, my feet feel an unpleasant sensation. When I take them off, there's a red stain on my socks.

I see. I bet I know what this is, I think and inspect them.

It looks like there was ketchup inside. I wouldn't do that myself, so someone else must have.

"Some people..." I mutter to myself, taking off my socks. Both of my slippers are full of ketchup.

They're not hot docks, you know, I think.

No, not hot docks, hot dogs. A dock is what you tie a boat to. A dog is man's best friend. A hot dog is a heated canine.

Even as I think I'm making no sense, I hold one of my ketchup-stained socks, walking down the corridor with my left foot still wearing its ketchup stained sock and my right foot bare. There should be slippers for guests somewhere.

"Huh? Mer? What's wrong?" Yakki calls out to me.

The lower half of Yakki's face is strangely relaxed. The upper half is just a little tense. From that expression, I become convinced that Yakki did it.

"I'm looking for slippers," I answer.

"Why? Huh? What happened to your socks there?"

"They got dirty somehow."

"How do you get them that dirty? You're weird, Mer. You're a little weird, you know that?"

"Am I?"

I decide to break up with Hakamada-kun.

When I tell him that after school, Hakamada-kun is flustered.

"Huh? Did I do something...?"

"You haven't done anything, Hakamada-kun," I tell him.

"Then why are you saying you want to break up?"

"I don't think this is right."

"Huh? What's not right?"

"How should I put this?" I say. "Umm, I think you probably do like me."

"Well, of course I do. That's why I asked you to go out with me. Wait, so you don't like me back then?"

"I think my feelings are very different from yours. I don't understand what it means to like someone in the first place."

"Then maybe you shouldn't have gone out with me in the first place?"

Hakamada-kun's face is bright red. He's really angry.

I can't blame him. I went out with him without much thought, and I'm regretting it. I think I've done him wrong. I've gotten him hurt.

It occurs to me that not wanting to hurt him was the reason I went out with him in the first place. That ended up hurting him more.

Hakamada-kun was the sort of person I could have a casual conversation with, and when he invited me out, we might have gone out and played with a few other people. Doing that was fun, but then he suddenly asked me out.

In the end, I probably didn't want to make things awkward by rejecting him. That was why I said yes. The result of that was that it got even more awkward, and the atmosphere now is downright unpleasant. I'll never be able to chat casually with Hakamada-kun again, I'm sure.

"I'm terrible," I say.

"You sure are," he agrees.

"I'm sorry." I bow my head.

Hakamada-kun says nothing.

I'm looking down. He has his left hand in his uniform pants. His right hand is clenched tightly, quivering.

If I say, *Let's not break up after all,* would that quell his anger? But I can't do that.

"Huh? So you broke up with Hakamada-kun then, Mer?" Yakki asks.

I respond that that's exactly what I did.

"The poor guy," Yakki says. "sad luck for Hakamada-kun."

I think she means bad luck. But I hold my tongue.

"I hope you learn from this, and don't do it again, Mer. People will hold it against you."

While responding, "Yeah," I wonder why Yakki would end up resenting me over what happened with Hakamada-kun.

Whenever I didn't understand things, I used to ask Dad about them. I never consulted Mom much, and I still don't. Now that I think of it, Mom is like Yakki in a way.

Yakki is usually floaty, smiley, and easy to talk to. But sometimes she can suddenly be cruel. Words so harsh they'll shock you will suddenly pop out of her mouth, and she'll go off on someone.

Then, when a little time passes, it's like she doesn't even remember what she said, and she acts like it never happened.

There have been many times when a little thing Mom says without meaning to—at least, I think she doesn't mean to—stabs into my chest, like a glass knife, leaving me in pain.

Whenever I talked to Dad about it, he said, *She doesn't mean any harm,* and patted me on the head.

She just happened to be in a bad mood, or something along those lines, I always think. *She has days like that.*

When was that time Dad and Mom were fighting?

"I'm saying it's not fair the way you act like that!" Mom shouted.

"You don't have to yell. I can hear you just fine."

"I'm always the villain. You may be fine with that, but I can't stand it."

"You're not the villain. I don't think you're bad. If one of us is bad here, it's me."

"You don't think that, and you know it!"

"I do think that."

"Well, then what's bad about you?"

"I'm making you angry. If I weren't bad, you wouldn't be upset with me."

Dad was a quiet person. He was always smiling, a little troubled, or looking worn out and tired.

The day Dad died, Mom sat down on a bench in the hospital, her face in her hands.

"How am I supposed to go on living without you...?"

I sat next to her, rubbing my Mom's back. I was sure Dad would have done the same.

"I'm here for you," I told her. "You're not alone, Mom."

Mom cried for a while, then nodded. After that, there were a bunch of things that happened that night, and I went into a dark room and watched the videos Dad had taken. Dad didn't appear in any of them.

In one video, I was running. Where was that field, anyway?

If I asked Mom, would she know? Mom probably knew. Mom must have been with us then.

I want to go to that place. The sunlight shines down strongly, and there's hardly any wind, and if I stay put, it's hot, but I can just run.

"You don't like pink, Merry?" Dad asks me.

"Yeah, not really," I say.

"What color do you like?"

"White, maybe? Oh, and blue!"

"Light blue, huh?"

The clothes Mom goes out and buys me on her own tend to be pink.

"You're a girl, so pink really is the cutest, right?" she always says.

Whenever she says that, and I get upset, Dad says helpfully, "Even if she is a girl, I think she can wear any color she wants."

I want to run.

Let's run.

I'm gonna run.

"Hey..." I hear a voice calling me.

Who could it be?

Dad, maybe? The voice sounds different.

I want to run more, so I pay it no mind, and I run.

"Hey, Merry..." I think it's a familiar voice.

I stop. Is it Michiki, maybe?

I turn back.

In the distance, there's someone. Not just one person. Michiki and the gang, maybe?

"Michiki? Mutsumi? Ogu?"

I raise my voice, calling out to them. I don't know if it's three people or not. They're too far off. Whatever the case, there's someone pretty far away, and they aren't moving.

"Mutsumi? Ogu? Michiki? Yakki? Dad? Mom?"

No matter how many times I call, they won't come. If it's not Michiki and the others, or Yakki, or Dad, or Mom...

I try to call everyone's names. Everyone...

Who? Who's everyone?

It won't come to me.

I can't remember.

Why?

Oh, right, it occurs to me. *If they won't come to me, I can just go to them.*

This time, I run towards them.

Run.

But no matter how much I run, I can't get closer to those people. I move forward and forward, but they don't get any bigger.

I get exhausted, and come to a stop.

Suddenly, there's a shadow cast.

I turn back, and some large, black thing flies overhead.

What is that?

I follow it with my eyes.

It vanishes over the horizon before I can figure it out.

I give up and look for those people.

They're not there. Not anywhere. They're gone.

I don't know in what direction. Where did I come from, and where was I going?

The grassy field stretches as far as the eye can see. The grass, the sky. There is nothing else.

"...I'm alone," I whisper.

My voice doesn't even sound hollow. It's kept pushed down inside my heart.

All...alone.

I mull over those words, chewing on them until they've lost all flavor, and then it finally occurs to me.

Oh.

I look around.

There's the sky, the grass, and nothing else, the same as ever.

I died, I realize. *That's why I'm alone.*

I feel like there was someone in the distance before, but it's just my imagination. I died, and ended up all alone, so there can't have been anyone.

Once you die, you lose yourself, and stop understanding anything, I'm sure.

But before that, I wanted to see them. That wish of mine may have made it feel like there was someone there.

I try to sit down. My body won't listen to me.

I lower my eyes.

I can't see my own hands. I have no arms, no legs, no body.

No nothing.

Oh, it's because I died—I think.

Because I died, there's nothing left of me.

But it's strange.

I can still think like this.

Am I really thinking?

Even though I no longer exist?

In this infinite field, with the sky so high...

Field?

Sky?

Where are either of those?

They're gone.

I see nothing.

Do I hear nothing because the wind isn't blowing?

I try to close my eyes. Nothing changes. Obviously.

I have no body. So I have no eyes.

The one thing I can do is think.

It's not clear if what I'm doing is thinking or not, but I think.

Think.

What should I think about?

I decide to count.

One. Two. Three. Four. Five. Six. Seven. Eight. Nine. Ten. Eleven. Twelve. Thirteen. Fourteen. Fifteen. Sixteen. Seventeen. Eighteen. Nineteen. Twenty. Twenty-one. Twenty-two.

Twenty-three. Twenty-four. Twenty-five. Twenty-six. Twenty-seven. Twenty-eight. Twenty-nine. Thirty. Thirty-one. Thirty-two. Thirty-three. Thirty-four. Thirty-five. Thirty-six. Thirty-seven. Thirty-eight. Thirty-nine. Forty. Forty-one. Forty-two. Forty-three. Forty-four. Forty-five. Forty-six. Forty-seven. Forty-eight. Forty-nine. Fifty. Fifty-one. Fifty-two. Fifty-three. Fifty-four. Fifty-five. Fifty-six. Fifty-seven. Fifty-eight. Fifty-nine. Sixty. Sixty-one. Sixty-two. Sixty-three. Sixty-four. Sixty...sixty... four. Five? Sixty...six...sixty...five? Six?

No, let me count. The numbers, please. If I don't, ah...

I'll disappear.

Disappear.

Disap...

"Merry."

There's a voice.

Someone's voice.

I want to see you.

Because this is the last time.

This is the end.

Before I vanish.

Everyone, please—

Who is everyone?

Merry? Merry...?
He held my hand.
Wh...what should I do...?
You don't have to do anything.
I don't need anything.
Because you've already done enough for me.
That's no lie.
I
was
happy
because I
wasn't alone.
You were
there for me.

Haru
I
Listen, I
Haru, I

What was it?
I
What was I trying to say again?

I forget

There were things I wanted to tell you
So many things
They're all spilling away, so goodbye
Oh, if this is goodbye
If I'm going far away

Everyone

I'm glad I was able to

"Hey, Geek."

I have a stupid grin on my pimply face, when Matt, the big guy who has spent more than five years mocking me, calls me that.

In that moment, I snap. I fly at him. My surprise attack is a success. I push Matt down. I get on top of him. I flail at his face.

My body is weak. I can't actually clobber Matt, so I'm flailing ineffectually.

Matt recovers from his shock. He easily pushes me off him. In no time, Matt is clobbering me, and his blows aren't nearly so ineffectual.

It hurts. I'm scared. I want him to spare me. But I don't beg for mercy. I defend myself desperately, and grit my teeth. I hold out until Matt's fierce assault stops.

Matt's fists start to hurt eventually, and he leaves, spewing profanities as he goes.

Keenesburg.

I lie on the side of the road on South Pine Street, alone, singing a little victory song to myself. I'm a geek, but I'm not weak. Or stupid. I'll get stronger, and I'll make my dream come true.

I study Japanese. My main study materials are anime and manga. Also, anisong and J-pop. Then I read Japanese novels. I study.

I was good at the sciences to begin with. Once I start studying Japanese on my own, I stop hating subjects in the humanities so much.

I run. I stretch. I do body-building. Train up my body.

I can't be a big guy like Matt. Still, I've got some muscle on me. No one wants to mess with me now.

I endure the solitude. I work my hardest. Finally, I set foot on Japanese soil as an exchange student. It's for a period of about a year.

Why couldn't I have been born in this country? Anyway, the country is well-suited to me. I'm an otaku and a geek, of course.

With my host family, the Hazakis, I feel a warm sort of familial love that I've never experienced with my real family.

In a Japanese high school, a place I have dreamed of attending, I'm able to make real friends for the first time.

I find love, too.

With a Japanese high school girl, a JK, Satsuki. Yes, I get myself a girlfriend with the same name as that girl in *Tonari no Totoro*.

I hold hands with Satsuki—

We walk al ong an emba nkment, cr oss a bri dge, go into a bo okst

"Jessie, your Japanese is really good," she says. "It's, like, so natural."

...Satsuki?

Jessie?

I ki ss Sa tsu ki.

It's a cute kiss, where only our lips touch.

...Who? Me? With Satsuki?

I seriously love Satsuki. I want to love her with all the sincerity I can muster, while still remaining true to myself.

Love Sa tsuki while re main ing true to my self…

I feel something is weird. Something is weird. The day I leave Japan draws closer.

Satsuki tells me, "I'm okay with a long-distance relationship."

I just repeatedly tell her I love her. Because I love Satsuki.

Finally, I return home. I have video chat sessions with Satsuki multiple times every day. We shoot the breeze. I feel happy just with that.

But when our chat sessions end, I feel hopelessly alone and sad. I want to hear Satsuki's voice again. I start wanting to see her face.

Just as I'm closing one session—because it's late in Japan, so Satsuki must need to get to sleep—I sense something is weird.

"Jessie, aren't you being a little cold lately?" Satsuki says, and when I apologize, she snaps at me.

Something is weird. It's wrong. Everything is wrong.

Who am I? I'm Jessie? I…

"Ageha, we'll be together forever." Takaya holds me tight and whispers in my ear.

I want him to hold me like this forever. Takaya's chin is pressed against my forehead.

Takaya doesn't shave properly every day, so when he moves, his beard scratches my forehead, and it hurts a little. I remember telling him to shave. He said okay, but he forgets after a few days. Eventually, I give up. I get used to it.

Now, I don't find this sensation so unpleasant. This time when Takaya and I are wrapped together in a blanket, it's hot, my head is fuzzy, I'm sleepy, but I can't get to sleep, and he is so very precious to me. I love him, and I want to ask him to kiss me, but I'm too embarrassed. I want Takaya to do it on his own. However, Takaya is sleeping.

Come on! I get angry. I try to sleep myself. When I do, Takaya's lips press against my forehead. They gradually move down. I accept them with my own lips.

While sharing a long kiss, I sense something is weird. Something is weird.

Takaya's warmth fades. He was warm until just a moment ago. Hot, even.

I'm still holding Takaya. I try to warm him up. I don't think it's in vain. I don't want to think that.

Rikimaru is nearby. Karatsu is here. Domiko is here. Taratsuna is here. Nobody is moving anymore.

The blood my comrades shed is now cold. I hear the buzzing of insects. Flies are gathering. I try to brush the flies away with my hand. But I can't shoo them all away. It's hard to move my hand at all. When I look, the flies have swarmed around my stomach, too.

I want to do something about that. I don't know what to do. *Takaya. Wake up, Takaya.* I want to call his name. My voice won't come out.

A fly lands on my lips. It's creeping around. The fly is trying to get inside me through them. I try to close my mouth. But it doesn't go so well. Instead, my eyes start to close. I sense something is weird. Something is weird.

"There is a way. Just one."

I realize something.

Even if I haven't been told directly, haven't I been given the key? What is the meaning behind why I, we, are taught MagicMissile, what is in some ways a unique spell, as our first spell?

I see now. So that was it.

"That's how it is, is it, Wizard Sarai?"

I say that to her directly. Sarai, the great elder of the mages' guild, simply smiles and says nothing.

I'm being told to think about it myself, I see. To open my own path. If I don't, I can never reach the true magic. The things I find that way will be my magic.

Even if I ask about that, Sarai won't confirm it. However, I am confident. I can finally see it. The path I must follow. I will walk the path where there is no path. That is my path.

"Yasuma," Sarai says to me. "You must not be hasty. Now look at me. Life is long, you see. You can take it slowly."

Naturally, that was my intention. Even as I sense something is weird, I finally have a clue. It's odd for me to say this myself, but I think I'm serious and studious. Once I became a volunteer soldier and a mage, I worked myself to the bone trying to master magic. I've acquired many spells.

I voice my opinions, and if I feel someone is wrong, I tell them so. Thanks to that, there have been times I've butted heads with others, and we've gone our own ways. However, there are always those who need me as a mage.

As a mage, and as a volunteer soldier, I've lived a life I can be proud of. I'm aware of that. Still, something is weird.

I decide to polish my Magic Missile. I am confident this will be my breakthrough. I'm still only halfway there. No, not even that; you could say I'm just starting out.

I can't fall yet. And yet, I feel something is weird.

"Live strong, Itsunaga. Strong..."

My mother is mostly covered in fallen leaves. I gathered them all myself.

Mother looks cold. She's shivering. That's why I think I have to warm her up.

I hold my mother's hand. Mother grips my hand back. Her grip soon weakens. Mother smiles.

My mother is dying. I know that, too. I've seen many creatures die, so I know what death is. My mother is about to die, and is leaving me a message to live strong.

Something weird is going on. Something is weird. Whether it is or not, Mother will die. Holding Mother's hand as she ceases to move, I swear to myself that I will never forget what the people of the village did to Mother and me.

Mother doesn't let out so much as a word of complaint. However, I am unable to forgive the people of the village. I simply cannot do it.

In my pocket I've stowed the short katana my mother had

me carry for protection. I resolve myself to avenge her with this blade. If this short katana cannot reach their throats, I will find myself a longer katana, and with it, I will pierce their hearts with a single stroke.

If I tell her that, my mother will surely stop me. So I will say nothing. Silently, I let Mother die in peace. Let her rest.

However, I think something weird is going on.

Something is weird.

Who am I? I'm Itsunaga? Even I don't know who I am anymore. Not for my part.

Names change. I don't care what I am called. I cast aside ten names, pick up a hundred, and possess a thousand.

Diha Gatt. That is but one of the thousand names I hold. However, it is a rather old name. Perhaps the oldest among them.

I am—

Jessie Smith.

Ageha.

Yasuma.

Itsunaga.

Diha Gatt.

Who am I?

The name doesn't matter. I have a thousand names. I have crossed thousands of lands.

Without destination? Something weird is going on. As I drift in search of sights unseen, something is definitely up with me.

Standing on the sheer cliffs of the inlet as the wind blows upward, I look out over the sea where bright green turns to blue, and then to deeper blues. Inhaling the suffocatingly strong scent of the sea, I narrow my eyes.

I look down to my own hands. My green hands. My thick fingers. My hard, durable claws.

I am a lone rat.

The Rat King.

I am

Je geha ha tsuna a sie yasu di su ma ie gatt mith ga dididididididiha gagagagagagagagagagagagagagagatt gaitsutsutsutsutsuna gayasusususususususumaa geageagegegegegegegegegeagehajessiejejejesiesmismismismismismismismithit hmemememememememememememememe merryryryrymememememememememememe jessiesmithagehayasuma itsunagadihagattratatatatatatatatat kingingingining

I mustn't go any further.

I am running
Run ning
Run

No field
No sky
No thing

Wh ere is this?
No one's he re

I'm al one

You're not alone, someone says.

Several people say it. They reach out. Touch me. Without hesitation. Violently. They force their way inside me. They go inside.

Stop. Don't go. Not inside me. Don't. Please.

"Merry!"

That's.

That's my.

"Merry!"

Call my name.

Call it more.

Tie me down.

Don't let go.

"Merry!"

"Merry!"

"Merry!"

Oh...

And so, I try to open my eyes.

Kuzaku came into the building.

"What the hell!" he yelled to the group. "Do those things plan to stay here even after dark?!"

Again and again, more times than he could count, Kuzaku had gone outside, and then come back in like this. He had to be exhausted. He was no doubt starving and thirsty. Even so, he couldn't stay put.

It was easy to understand why. Haruhiro felt the same. It was hard to keep quiet about it. But he couldn't move away from her side.

Yume sat with one knee up by the broken entrance with no door. Though she had a katana in hand, her fingers were just barely wrapped around the hilt.

Yume remained looking down the whole time. Even if he called out to her, she might not respond. That was the feeling Haruhiro got.

Shihoru was in a similar state. She was sitting next to Haruhiro, hanging her head and not moving.

The birds were still making a terrible racket. Taking turns standing on the edge of the hole in the ceiling, there were more than ten crows, and they were as noisy as ever.

Kuzaku kicked the ground, then crouched. A moment later, he said, "What do we do?"

Haruhiro opened his mouth to say something. Nothing came out.

He licked his lips. They hurt a little. His lips were dry and cracked.

Haruhiro ultimately just said, "Nothing yet."

"Okay, then."

Kuzaku tried to stand up. Were his legs not working? He ended up collapsing.

As for Haruhiro, it wasn't that he'd just been watching and doing nothing else. It had taken a lot of courage, but he had checked Merry's state and the state of Jessie, who had turned into something like a thin, leather doll, and he'd done it not once, but many times.

It was especially terrifying to touch Jessie. There was no warmth in Jessie's skin, and it didn't feel moist, but it wasn't bone dry, either.

Haruhiro tried lifting up Jessie's left wrist. It had weight, like it was supposed to. But not the weight of a human. Was it just as it appeared, and Jessie was nothing but skin and bones now? There was no way he was alive, but he didn't have the stench of death, either. That meant he wasn't rotting.

On that point, she was the same.

She had died. Or should have. Haruhiro had been there the moment it happened.

In this present moment, too, she wasn't alive. He'd confirmed that himself. She had no pulse. Her heart wasn't moving. Her body temperature probably wasn't even all that different from the ambient temperature. Despite that, rigor mortis had not set in. She wasn't rotting.

There was one other thing he had checked, since it had caught his attention.

In humans, if they were alive, the heart was always beating, creating a constant flow of blood through their body. If the heart stopped, naturally, the flow of blood would, too. What would happen then?

Well, blood was acted on by gravity. If a person was lying face-up, the blood would gather into the back of the body. That was evident even looking at a corpse from the outside. It was called postmortem lividity, and that section turned purple.

Haruhiro tried to lift her head up. In order to do that, he had to move Jessie, who had his left wrist pressed up against the wound on her shoulder. Haruhiro gently undid the cloth tying Jessie and her together.

He doubted his eyes. There was a gash-like wound on Jessie's left wrist. However, her shoulder was clean.

The massive wound that could fairly have been said to have killed her had now vanished completely. He didn't see any of the copious amounts of blood that should have bled from Jessie's wound, either. Even the cloth, which should have been dark with blood, was dry and not particularly dirty.

With a groan, Haruhiro lifted up her head, moving aside her hair to look at the nape of her neck.

Perhaps this result should have been a given.

There was no sign of postmortem lividity there.

What exactly did this mean? She wasn't alive. However, he couldn't say she was dead, either. There was no way she could just stay like this. There had to be some sort of change that would occur.

What kind of change? He couldn't predict that. That was obvious. There was no way he could possibly predict it.

Haruhiro was hopeful it would be a good change. At the same time, he was frightened. Something unbelievable might be about to happen. It might already be happening.

No matter what sort of change it was, he had no choice but to accept it. But, in the end, would he be able to?

Awooooooooooooooooooooooooooooooooooooo...

"Whoa!" Kuzaku leapt to his feet.

Yume turned to look outside, too.

"Haruhiro-kun..." Shihoru called out, and Haruhiro nodded.

He hadn't forgotten. Jessie told them. When the sun went down, the vooloos would come.

Yume stood on one knee, readying her katana. Someone rushed into the building. Yume let them pass without intercepting them. It wasn't one of the carrion eaters known as a vooloo. It was Setora with a head staff, followed by Kiichi the gray nyaa.

Setora didn't even look at Yume or Kuzaku as she rushed over to Haruhiro. "Haru!"

"Yeah," was all Haruhiro said in response.

Setora leaned the head staff against the bars, then came to a stop standing in front of Haruhiro. She took a breath.

Kiichi nuzzled up against Setora's shins, meowing with a *nyaa* sound.

"Where've you been all this time?" Shihoru asked.

"Searching," Setora responded curtly, taking a fist-sized object out of her pocket.

It wasn't just a matter of size. It was shaped like a clenched fist, too. Was it metal? It looked hard, and seemed to have a considerable amount of weight to it. It looked like there were a number of holes in it. A pale blue light leaked out from them.

Haruhiro looked at the object. That was all he did. It didn't draw his interest in the least. No matter what it was, honestly, he didn't care.

"This is a pseudo-soul vessel," Setora explained on her own. "Enba's pseudo-soul is inside. It's what you might call the true body of a flesh golem. The necromancer ties a pseudo-soul to a golem made by stitching dead bodies together. I was born into the House of Shuro, and so I have been messing around with the dead bodies of people and animals for as long as I can remember. Even in the village, the House of Shuro is viewed as unsettling. I was often mocked as stinky, too."

She paused.

"The truth is, a necromancer hardly ever deals with rotting corpses. In fact, a meticulously washed corpse is cleaner and less smelly than a living human. Besides, when used properly, bones, muscles, blood vessels, and organs are truly beautiful. When you see a flesh golem made by stitching these things together begin to move, it's a moving sight, to say the least. However, once I built Enba, I could no longer motivate myself to work on another golem. The necromancers of the House of Shuro make golems, destroy them, then make new ones. They repeat that their entire lives, aiming to heighten their craft. I was satisfied with Enba. Not that the members of my house ever understood that. It was seen as eccentric for a woman of the House of Shuro to take up raising nyaas. It seems I'm something of an oddball."

Haruhiro nodded vaguely. If it weren't for the current situation, he'd probably have listened to Setora properly. But he couldn't now. He didn't want to hear it. He couldn't listen. To be frank, he had other concerns.

"Haru." Setora tucked the pseudo-soul vessel back in her pocket. Kiichi stared up at her. "You love that woman, I see."

"Wha—" His face twitched, and he was lost for words. Why would she say that, out of nowhere?

Why here? Why now?

Awoooooooooooooooooooooooooooooooooo...!

The vooloos were howling.

Haruhiro looked up to the hole in the ceiling. At some point, all the crows had vanished. He looked down, blinked twice, and took a breath.

"It's one-sided," he said.

I can't lie, he thought. *That's the one thing I can't do.*

"It's my...one-sided feelings, you could say. That's not really any of—"

"It's fine." Setora crouched down, reaching out with her right hand and covering Haruhiro's mouth. Then, for some reason, she smiled a little, and said, "I understand. But listen, Haru," she continued in a different tone of voice.

Setora's hand was quivering. She put more strength into it.

"The dead don't come back."

Haruhiro could say nothing in return. Not because Setora had his mouth covered. He could easily fix that. Haruhiro was suspicious.

Am I having a dream? A dream in which the dead come back to life? Even though death is the end for people?

With that one statement from Setora, his convenient dream broke down, and he awoke. That was how it felt now.

Setora pulled back her right hand, wrapping it in her left and gripping it. "The golem was, in a way, a product of compromise. The people who later came to be known as necromancers had originally been attempting to resurrect the dead. The acquisition of a relic made it so they were able to create pseudo-souls, and they continued their attempts after the creation of the golem. However, they've never succeeded, not even once. Death is an irreversible phenomenon. It's not just people—no living thing can return from death. Even if that woman starts breathing again, the way I see it, it won't be the sort of revival you hope for. The woman who comes back may be a different person from the one who died. I hope she's not some unknown monster, at least."

Haruhiro said nothing.

"Still, if she's adorably loyal like a golem, that'll be something. But what will you do if she isn't?"

"What will I...?"

"No," Setora said. "There's nothing you can do. You will have to recognize and accept it all."

"I...know that."

"Really? Can you hold your head high and say you're prepared to do that, Haru?"

If he was prepared for it, he should have held his head high and nodded immediately. But he couldn't.

"If you can't do it..." Setora softened her tone and spoke quietly. "...then there is something you must do right now."

"Something...I must do?"

"Yes, that's right. I'm sure there's still time. Pierce that woman's head and heart with your stiletto. End it like that. If you can't do it, I can do it for you. I'm used to shouldering others' bad karma. I can do it without hesitation. I'll do it in an instant."

There's still time. Is there? I have to do it. Me. With my own hands. That, or have Setora do it. No, if anyone does it, it has to be me. But is that necessary? It's not. Resolve. Yeah. If I just have the resolve. If I can say I'm fine, no matter what happens.

"Urgh..." There was a groan.

It wasn't from Haruhiro. Or Setora. It wasn't from Shihoru, or Yume, or Kuzaku, either.

It was Merry.

Merry's limbs all thrust outwards. It wasn't just her arms and legs. Her neck and torso bent back like a bow, too.

"Merry...!" Haruhiro jumped on her. His head was soon knocked back.

"Arghhhhhhhhhhhhhhhhhhhhhhhhhhhhhhh!" he screamed.

It was dark so he couldn't see well, but something was flowing out of Merry's mouth, and likely other parts of her, too. What? What was coming out of Merry?

"Ugh..." Haruhiro covered his mouth despite himself, and held his breath.

This stench.

Blood?

Could this be blood, maybe? It was similar to the smell of blood. No, but it was more raw.

"What...?!" Setora backed away.

"M-merry-chan?!" Yume cried.

"Merry-san!" Kuzaku yelled.

"Eek!" Shihoru let out a little scream.

What was this? What the hell was this? Haruhiro ended up kneeling with his left hand on the ground. The blood, or whatever it was, he didn't really know, but the liquid that was coming out of Merry got Haruhiro's left hand wet, and then his knees. There were copious amounts of it.

"Aguh, goh, guh, gah, gwuh, gwah, agah, haack, bleurgh..." Merry let out bizarre sounds instead of her voice as she continued to vomit the liquid substance.

What now? What should I do? I can't just do nothing. I have to make some move. I've got to do something. I mean, she looks like she's suffering.

"M-merry...!"

Haruhiro took a bold step forward, hugging Merry around the shoulders. He wanted to stop it. Stop the liquid from coming out. But was it okay to make it stop? Could he stop it? How?

The liquid just kept coming out from inside Merry. Merry was already soaked with it. Haruhiro was, too. His hands, his arms, his legs, they were all drenched. It had splashed up as far as his face. This liquid was probably not just ordinary blood. Or was it even blood?

Haruhiro pressed down on Merry's right shoulder with his left hand, reaching out to her cheek with his right hand. It wasn't just her mouth, after all. The liquid substance seemed to be flowing out of her nose and eyes, too. Haruhiro tried to wipe it away. It was meaningless. It kept on coming out. Was there a bottomless reservoir of it? It never stopped, not even for a moment. But he couldn't help but wipe it. Because it wasn't possible for him to just do nothing.

"Merry, can you hear me?! Merry! It's me, Haruhiro! Merry!"

He wanted to do something, but couldn't do anything about the liquid substance. It was impossible to stop it when it was gushing out like this.

"Merry! Merry! Merry!" Haruhiro kept calling out to her.

Merry's whole body was rigid, and she might start flailing around again at any moment. This had to be tremendously hard on her. She was probably suffering.

If she was suffering, that meant she was in a state where she could suffer. In that case, weren't they almost there? Almost where, though? It was hard to explain. But, probably, it would just be a little longer.

Haruhiro held Merry and shouted. "It's going to be okay! You don't have to worry! I'm here! I—we—are here! Merry, we're with you!"

Your body is here, but maybe you're still somewhere else. Somewhere my voice can't reach. You may not even be able to hear my measly voice. In that case, I'll keep shouting until it reaches you. I'll roar, let my voice echo, so that it reaches you. I may not be able to take your hand, wherever you are, and lead you back here. But, in that case, I'll shout for you as loud as I can, and pull you towards me.

"Merry. Merryyyy!"

Haruhiro hugged Merry tighter. He tried shouting her name one more time. His voice had long since gone hoarse. He didn't care if he ruined his throat. He'd call her name as long as he had to.

Merry inhaled. Up until now, all she had done was spew the liquid substance.

She started coughing. "Ha...ru?"

Through a great deal of coughing, he was certain he heard Merry say that.

Then she managed, "Haru. It was you, Haru?"

What was Merry thinking had been Haruhiro? Haruhiro didn't know. But it didn't matter.

"Yeah! It's me, Merry. Haruhiro. You know me. You can hear me, right? Merry. You came back. Merry! Merry...!"

Merry nodded. It looked like her coughs were subsiding. Her breathing was still extremely ragged. Regardless, Merry was clearly conscious. Clearly, in a way that couldn't be misunderstood. Merry had called Haruhiro's name. She understood what Haruhiro was saying.

Which meant...?

This is unbelievable.

No, I can believe it.

What words can possibly express this feeling? "We did it"? "Thank goodness"? Should I say, "Welcome back"? "I've been waiting"? "Thank you for coming back to us"? "I missed you"? They're all true,

*but even if I said them all, it wouldn't be enough. But if Merry's
with us, that's more than enough.*

Awoooooooo! Awoo! Awoo! Awoooooooo! Awoooo!

"Haruhiro!" Kuzaku shouted. "It's those vooloo things!"

"Vooloos," Merry said clearly. She tried to get up.

Haruhiro immediately tried to hold her down. "Merry,
not yet—"

"Now isn't the time to say that."

She was absolutely right. Now wasn't the time to be telling
her she wasn't ready yet. Haruhiro helped Merry to her feet.

Merry tried to walk, then stumbled. Her head staff was leaned
up against the nearby bars.

Merry took it in hand. "For equipment," she murmured, then let
out a low groan and shook her head. "It would help to have a shield.
A bow and arrows, too. They should still be in the storehouse..."

"Merry...?"

"We need to hurry."

Merry crouched down, searching through Jessie's body, which
was not so much a corpse as a cast-off shell. What exactly was she
doing? Before he had time to ask, Merry stood up.

"I'll show you to the storehouse. It's really close. Come on."

"Er... Uh, okay."

Haruhiro had some doubts, but he cast them aside. Now
wasn't the time to talk about them.

Setora and Kiichi were by the entrance, as well as Yume and
Shihoru.

Kuzaku was outside. He was a little way away, his large katana shining with white light. He must have cast the light magic spell Saber on it.

Awoooooooo! Awooo! Awoo! Awooooooo!

They were close. The howls of the vooloos.

"They're huge!" Kuzaku cried out.

Was he talking about a vooloo? Where were they? Haruhiro couldn't see them yet.

"O Light, may Lumiaris's divine protection be upon you. Protection."

Merry used light magic. A shining hexagram appeared on Haruhiro and everyone else's left wrists.

"Hahhhhh!" Kuzaku swung his large katana. There was a flash of white light, and...

It was just a glimpse, but I think I saw one. A vooloo. Is that it? But seriously, isn't it kind of huge...?

"Kuza—" he began.

"Whoa...?!"

The shadow of the apparent vooloo swallowed Kuzaku. No, did it jump on him and push him down? Haruhiro couldn't even take a step. Yume, Shihoru, and Setora were the same.

It was only Merry. Leaving behind Haruhiro and the others, Merry rushed in.

"O Light, may Lumiaris's divine protection be upon you..." Merry unleashed a blinding light towards the vooloo that was on top of Kuzaku. "Blame!"

It let out a yelp, its entire body shuddering, and, though it was only for an instant, this time they got a clear look at it.

It was covered in fur, and probably blackish in color. Blackish brown, blackish gray, or something like that. It was a carrion-eating wolf.

A wolf? Haruhiro thought incredulously. *How is that a wolf? What part of it? Wolves aren't that big, right? They're more lean, aren't they? Isn't that thing too solid? But I feel like the shape of its head was dog-like. It was like a wolf. But taken as a whole, it gave off a very different impression. Rather than a wolf, that thing was like a bear.*

The moment the word "bear" came to mind, he remembered. Jessie had been talking about them.

"East of the Kuaron Mountains, there are vooloos that are bigger than the mist panthers in Thousand Valley. They're the size of bears," he'd said.

Bears.

That was it. He'd said "bears"!

"Geddoff!" Kuzaku pushed the vooloo away, getting out from beneath it. At almost exactly the same time, maybe immediately before, maybe right after, Merry wound up and slammed her head staff into the vooloo's face. It looked like that gave the vooloo pause.

Merry cried, "Haru!" as she took off running. Was she heading for the storehouse, or whatever it was?

"We're moving!" Haruhiro said, then immediately it occurred to him, *This is bad. I'm not making decisions myself. I'm just going with the flow. What's the point in me even existing? No, my reason for existing isn't important here.*

"Ahh, damn it!" Kuzaku cried. "Thanks, Merry-san! I'm glad you're okay! Zahhhhhh!" He struck the vooloo with his large katana, then turned and ran.

"Go, everyone! Go!" Haruhiro swung his arms around, urging them on.

Setora and Kiichi, Yume, Shihoru, and finally Kuzaku followed after Merry. Haruhiro followed behind Kuzaku.

The vooloos were coming.

Awoooooooo! Awoo! Awoooooo! Awooo! Awooo!

There were vooloos howling here and there. How many of them were there? There were many. How could there be several of those bear-like things? No, before he worried about the other vooloos, he had to worry about the one from before.

Fuh, hah, hoh, hah, hah, hahh, hah, hahh.

He could hear its breath as it closed in. The vooloo from before made a frenzied charge. It would catch them. It was coming to attack.

"Ru...!"

Haruhiro let out an odd exclamation as he jumped to the side, rolled, and got back up.

That was close! Its claws, or something, grazed him!

The vooloo let out a dissatisfied growl, crouching back its large body, like it was preparing for something. Was it?

Oh, crap, oh, crap, oh, crap!

Haruhiro ran. He ran as fast as he could. But he felt like he couldn't hope to beat it on speed.

Look. See? The vooloo's already this close.

It was dark, so he couldn't see it that well, though. Its eyes were shining.

It's close. It's too fast, way too fast. It's gonna get me.

"Eagh...!"

He tried to get away somehow. Did he not make it in time? The next thing he knew, he was being crushed. There was an intense animal smell. He couldn't breathe. Was he going to get eaten? Devoured?

"Take thiiiis...!" Kuzaku yelled.

Was Kuzaku turning back to make a strike on the vooloo that was trying to eat Haruhiro?

The vooloo yelped, but it didn't let Haruhiro go.

Kuzaku shouted, "Hey, you!" and slashed the vooloo again. "What do you think you're doing to Haruhiro? Get off! I'll kill you! Die, you damn bear!" He repeatedly hit it with his large katana.

No, I don't think this thing's a bear, Haruhiro reflected. *Or is it a bear? Does it matter?*

Finally, the vooloo got off Haruhiro.

Immediately, Kuzaku pulled him to his feet. "Haruhiro, are you okay?!"

"Yeah, somehow..."

"This is bad news. I can't cut that thing. Its fur's kind of—Oh...?!"

Kuzaku was knocked back. The vooloo had charged in again. Kuzaku, however, instinctively defended himself with his large katana. He managed to dig in and not to get knocked over somehow.

Awoooooooooooooo! The vooloo was about to pounce on Kuzaku.

Haruhiro drew his stiletto. He hadn't even had a weapon ready before now.

What the hell am I even doing?

He grabbed onto the vooloo that was about to charge Kuzaku again, wrestling with it and stabbing his stiletto into it. He stabbed and stabbed. He was definitely stabbing it like he meant to, and the vooloo was twisting around because it didn't like it, but—this wasn't working, was it?

The fur. This oily, tough fur was the culprit. The matted fur itself wasn't that hard, but it was dense and layered, forming something like a cushion. With something as short as his stiletto, Haruhiro could stab it in to the hilt, and the best it might manage was to pierce that fur cushion.

This was even more trouble than the guorella's shell-like skin. If he was going to do this right, would he have to target the eyes, or something like that?

The vooloo let out a howl as it raised its upper body. It was standing on its hind legs.

"Oh?!" Haruhiro yelped.

Is this thing not really a wolf, but actually a bear? I mean, when this thing stands, it's really huge!

"Whoa?! Ohhhh?!" Kuzaku looked surprised.

Haruhiro desperately clung to the vooloo's back. But the vooloo bayed and shook its body violently, so he couldn't hold on.

This is bad.

I can't do this.

I don't have the strength.

He was shaken off, went flying, and instead of the ground, he struck the wall of a building. The wall wasn't able to stop Haruhiro, so he broke right through it.

"Ungh... Guh..."

Huh?

It's...bright?

"Yikes!" That was...Yume's voice?

Haruhiro was on his back. He'd hit his head hard on his way through the wall, apparently. Because of that, he was a bit shaken up.

Looking around, he eventually found Yume. Shihoru, too. And Setora, and Kiichi.

Oh, so that was it. The storehouse. This was the storehouse. That made sense. That was why the lights were on. That was why Yume was here, Shihoru was here, Setora was here, Kiichi was here, and, of course, Merry was, too.

"...Huh?"

How bizarre.

For some reason, it looked like Merry wasn't wearing any clothes.

What was this? An illusion? It had to be. After all, there was no reason she would be getting naked here.

"Haru...!"

Merry flew over to him. Not literally, of course. That was a given. Merry couldn't fly. But she was fast.

When a naked Merry hugged him, Haruhiro thought maybe this might be heaven. Nah, probably not. There was no heaven, right? But in that case, was this reality...?

"Hey, you!" Setora threw a greenish coat at Merry. "Put that on, at least!"

"Ah...!" With Haruhiro's head still in her lap, Merry took that green coat-like garment and covered her breasts. "Th-this is, um, my clothes were soaked, so I was getting changed..."

"O-oh." Haruhiro shut his eyes tight. "...Yeah. I won't look. No matter what."

"Meow! Kuzakkun's in trouble!" Yume shouted.

"We've gotta support him!" Shihoru yelled.

Yume and Shihoru are making a fuss for some reason. No, not for some reason. Kuzaku's taking on a vooloo on his own. Me, meanwhile? What is this? Is it okay for me to be using Merry's lap as a pillow, shutting my eyes tight while she changes? It isn't, right?

"Er, um... Haru, I've got the upper half on, so..."

"Oh, ohh..."

Haruhiro opened his eyes and hurriedly sat up. He peeked at Merry.

Merry was in the middle of standing up. She had the green coat on, like she ought to. Only her legs were bare. She said she'd covered her top. What about her bottom...?

He shook his head. Even if she was naked down below, what did it matter? Besides, if she had a change of clothes, yeah, she was going to want to change. Her previous outfit was a total mess at this point. Honestly, Haruhiro wanted to get changed himself.

Yume was carrying a bow, and had a quiver full of arrows slung over her shoulder. Setora had a spear in hand. She was carrying a square shield, too.

Shihoru was carrying a shield as well, but not for herself, so she probably meant to pass it to Kuzaku.

Looking at it again, small though it was, this building was most definitely a storehouse. The racks were lined with swords and spears, and a number of shields were leaned up against the walls.

There were bows. There were arrows. There was a shelf with cloth and pieces of clothing on it. It wasn't clear what was inside them, but there were jars. It wasn't just lamps hanging from the rafters. There were some other things he couldn't readily identify there, too.

Haruhiro looked in Merry's direction despite himself. He immediately averted his eyes. Merry was crouched down, fumbling around inside her coat. She was probably putting clothes on.

"Nuwah! Zwah! Seahhhh!" Kuzaku was fighting the vooloo by himself.

"R-right!" Haruhiro returned to his senses, but before he could give any orders...

"The shield!" Setora shouted, hurrying Shihoru.

"Right...!" Shihoru responded immediately, heading out through the hole Haruhiro had busted in the wall. Yume followed after her.

Haruhiro slapped his left cheek with his left hand. *Get it together,* he told himself. He followed after Yume. Setora brought Kiichi and went with him.

When he looked, Shihoru had just finished shouting, "Kuzaku-kun...!" and throwing the shield. The shield rolled to Kuzaku's feet. Kuzaku glanced down at it, but that was all. It looked like he didn't have the breathing room to pick it up.

Kuzaku closed in on the vooloo, shouting and swinging his large katana. The large katana struck the vooloo's left shoulder, but he couldn't cut it, after all.

Kuzaku pulled back his large katana. "Hiyaahh...!"

He swung it down. The vooloo took a blow to the top of the head, but it just stumbled and backed away. The cushioning from its fur was a thing to be feared. What were they even supposed to do about it?

"You dolt, don't slash! Thrust!" Setora shouted.

She didn't just shout that. She raced towards the vooloo. Her spear outstretched, she rammed it into its throat. Incredibly, it stabbed in properly.

Setora let the spear go without hesitation, jumping back. "Get in there, you idiot!"

"Rarrrghhhh!"

Kuzaku charged at the vooloo. When Kuzaku went on the attack, unleashing his combat instincts all at once, he was violent to the point of being a little scary. And that was how it was now.

Kuzaku slammed his whole body straight into the vooloo. His large katana stabbed deep into its chest. Surprisingly, by that point Setora had already turned back to head for the storehouse.

"Haru!" When he heard his name and turned, a spear was tossed his way.

Why? he questioned, but Haruhiro instinctively caught it.

"You, too, hunter!" Setora threw Yume a spear as well, and took one for herself. "Come on!"

Even as Haruhiro thought, *I'm a moron, indecisive, incompetent, useless, and beyond all help,* he put away his stiletto and readied the spear.

He'd probably never used a spear before. But so what?

Kuzaku shouted, "Get back for now!" as Setora and Yume rushed in, each trying to get there first.

The one thrust Kuzaku had gotten in had been especially effective. The vooloo was completely on the back foot.

Saying that Haruhiro's, Setora's and Yume's spears were going to skewer it was a bit of an exaggeration, but all three of their spears stabbed into it wonderfully. The vooloo bent backwards in pain, but twisted its body just before it would have ended up on its back, so it fell on its side. It might have wanted to get on all-fours, but it looked like the four spears and Kuzaku's large katana, which were jammed in its throat, chest, and other places, were getting in the way.

"Out of the way!" Kuzaku, who had temporarily fallen back, jumped on the vooloo in a frenzy. He tore his large katana free and immediately stabbed. He pierced through it.

The mouth. Kuzaku rammed his large katana in the vooloo's mouth. That wasn't all.

"Raaarrrgh!" He twisted his large katana with brute force, pulling it up. The large katana bisected the vooloo's head from inside. No matter how tough of a beast it was, that had to be a lethal blow.

Haruhiro was relieved. Then, as if to tell him off for being too naive, Setora gave the gray nyaa some order. "Kiichi!"

He really was being naive. So naive, he had to wonder what had gotten into him. There were still vooloos howling all over the place, weren't there? This was hardly over. They hadn't overcome them yet. If they hadn't gotten out of this yet, what was he acting relieved for?

Merry left the storehouse, her head staff in one hand, a lamp in the other. That green coat, which didn't look priestly in the slightest was a fresh new look for her, and Haruhiro couldn't take his eyes off her.

He could only be exasperated with himself for that. There was something seriously wrong with him. He wasn't managing to do anything a leader should. Wasn't Setora acting far more like a leader? Was he in a slump or something? Was that it?

No, how could he call this a slump? He hadn't been cut out to be a leader to begin with. He'd never once been a good leader. Still, he'd had no choice but to do it, so he'd done what he could to the best of his ability, hadn't he?

If he was going to call this a slump, he was in a perpetual slump. It was normal for him to be in a slump, and he'd never be able to get out of it for the rest of his life.

He was dull, but he had to think.

Setora had given Kiichi some sort of order. It looked like Kiichi had gone off somewhere. Setora probably meant to have Kiichi look for an escape route for them.

Merry was carrying a lamp. Was that okay? The light seemed like it would stand out. But vooloos were nocturnal, right? They could see in the dark. If the party couldn't see, they were at a disadvantage in the darkness. It was better to have the light.

Anyway, for now they had to run. To get away from here.

He was an uninspiring leader, and there were far more things he didn't know or couldn't do than otherwise, but he couldn't whine about that, and since he couldn't get out of this alone, yeah, he'd have to borrow everyone else's strength.

"Setora! Which way should we go?!" he shouted.

"Wait." Setora made a sharp noise with the gap between her teeth. She closed her eyes, turning her head around.

It was faint, but there was a slight, *Nyaa.*

Which direction had it come from? Haruhiro couldn't decide. It seemed Setora heard it. She opened her eyes, pointing to the left.

"This way, for now. I can't guarantee it's safe, but—"

"Good enough. Kuzaku, take point!"

"'Kay!" Kuzaku picked up the shield and nodded.

"Setora, stay by my side and give directions."

"Okay, understood."

"Yume, stay in the back."

"Meow!"

"Merry, you..." He came close to muddling his words. He felt like he might cry. What good would that do? He just had to do as usual. To think, he was still able to give Merry directions as usual. "You protect Shihoru, and stay in front of Yume!"

Without missing a beat, Merry replied, "Sure!"

"Shihoru, conserve your magic," Haruhiro added. "We don't know what's out there."

His voice was halfway to tears.

"Okay!" Shihoru replied quickly. Her voice was tearful, too.

"Okay, let's go!"

Haruhiro and the party took off running.

He could hear the howling of vooloos. He sensed them moving around, but just how many vooloos were there, and where were they? He had no grasp on that whatsoever.

Setora frequently said, "This way!" and "That way!" giving directions. Haruhiro just followed them, even though he felt like his whole body was being torn up by a sense of powerlessness. While he couldn't shake it off just by accepting it had always been this way, he was able to endure it.

Looking back, it wasn't like there had been absolutely no times when things seemed to be going well. It only happened occasionally, though. Most of the time, it didn't go so well.

Even if he got results, he never got a perfect score of one hundred out of one hundred. It was always, *I should have done this,* or, *I should have done it this way, but I just can't.* He would think he needed to fix his shortcomings, but he'd also think it was a pain, too, and wouldn't commit to it.

The score he gave himself was always below fifty points. Forty-seven or forty-eight points, maybe.

"It looks like we can get out!" Setora shouted.

This is when I really need to get my act together, thought Haruhiro.

"Man, do you have any fun living like that?" He thought he heard that idiot Ranta's voice, and it made him sick.

If you're asking if it's fun or not, it's not like it's ridiculously fun or anything, he retorted silently. *But you'd be surprised; it's actually a little fun. Not that you'd understand that, Ranta. When you live like me, there are no intense ups and downs. Instead you get pretty happy or sad over the little things. I'm fine if someone wants to call it a boring way of life. I can't help that. This is who I am. I can only live as myself.*

It looked like he'd gotten back to his usual self. Because of what had happened with Merry, he'd uncharacteristically lost his composure. Despite that, Merry had come back somehow, and Kuzaku, Yume, Shihoru, Setora, and Kiichi were all fine, too. He should probably consider this lucky.

Lucky, because Haruhiro, who was the leader despite all his faults, had been useless. Given that, it wouldn't have been strange if this had turned into an even bigger disaster.

He was fine with a score of fifty out of one hundred. Even a score in the forties wasn't bad. Looking for a sixty was asking too much. He'd do his best to avoid scoring lower than forty. He himself was around a fifty, but he wanted to make it so everyone was able to score a sixty, maybe even a seventy.

Somehow, he wanted to make this party a sixty or better. He'd contribute what he could to make that happen. That was Haruhiro's job as a leader.

Know your place. Don't overextend yourself. If you lose your balance because of doing so, it defeats the purpose. Just calm down for now. Look. Listen. Feel. Use everything you can. Especially your head. Even if it's repetitive and there's no progress, don't lose interest. Keep doing it without getting tired of it. There is something more important than you moving forward, step by step, yourself. Move your comrades forward. I think it would be fine to have larger ambitions, like "I want to do something big," or "I want people to think I'm incredible," but in the end, I have hardly anything like that in me. Wishes like "I want to see new sights," or "I want to stand on the shoulders of giants" have nothing to do with me.

But for my comrades, I can try reasonably hard.

I don't hate that about me. I do my best for my comrades. That's my core. If I lose sight of it, I can't keep walking. No, I can't even stay standing.

They got out of the village, joining back up with Kiichi as soon as they entered the fields.

Awooo! Awoo! Awoooo! Awooooo!

The howling of the vooloos was coming from behind them... or at least that was what Haruhiro thought, but he couldn't be sure. If it was true, they could run away like this. He really hoped that was the case.

"Kiichi!" Setora sent the nyaa out again.

Kiichi ran ahead of Haruhiro and the party. If there were vooloos up ahead, he would alert them.

"I can still kill another one or two!" Kuzaku was winded, but he sounded reliable.

"Merry, put out the lamp!" Haruhiro shouted.

"Got it!" Merry called and put it out.

The vooloos had good night vision. That said, having a bright lamp lit out in the middle of the field was like telling them their prey was right here.

There were a lot of clouds, and no moon. There were few stars. It was a suffocating sort of darkness. Even so, once his eyes adjusted, Haruhiro could just barely make out the outlines of his comrades beside him.

The howls of the vooloos were not close. They'd gotten further away—or so he thought.

"They are carrion eaters, after all..." Setora muttered.

She had to be talking about the vooloos. The vooloos weren't that interested in living prey like the party to begin with, so they might not be that fixated on them. Ideally, that would be the case. That said, that was only his hope, so they couldn't let their guards down.

"Yume, she's thinkin' there aren't no more of them around here!"

If Yume felt that way, it might be true. But no, no, they couldn't relax.

Stay cautious. To the point of being cowardly, if anything.

"Shihoru?! You're not tired, are you?!" Haruhiro couldn't see her very well when he turned back to ask.

"I'm still okay!" Shihoru replied.

Immediately, Merry added, "It's okay!"

If Shihoru was pushing herself beyond her limit, Merry would have stopped her rather than say it was okay.

Setora let out a snorting laugh. "You people…" she started to say, then closed her mouth.

"Huh? What?"

"No," Setora said, and shook her head.

Kuzaku's steps were heavy. It looked like he was having a pretty hard time. It was a bit late to be noticing, but Kuzaku must have been struggling all along. Haruhiro wanted to let him rest, but not yet. Even if he was going to let him rest eventually, now wasn't the time. Though, that said, it would be a problem if he collapsed on them.

"Let's drop our pace," Haruhiro said.

"'Kay!" Kuzaku stopped running, and started to walk with long strides.

The howling of the vooloos was a good distance away now. Could they make it?

Whew. Haruhiro let out a deep sigh. Whenever there was an opening, he couldn't help but loosen up. That frailty was his greatest enemy.

He was his own greatest enemy. It was ironic that when his own, weak self was the enemy, that made him actually pretty frightening.

He came close to thinking about Ranta, but banished the thought. Why would he think about that guy? They weren't comrades anymore. But…

Maybe I don't think that? I don't believe he completely betrayed us.

Forget about it. I can say, at the very least, that thinking about him isn't going to do any good right now.

I want to relax. Honestly, from the bottom of my heart, I just want to take it easy and relax. To eat something good, then to sleep soundly. For just one day—no, even half a day—I want to spend my time like that. It's an incredible luxury. I know that. I have to put aside even dreaming about it for now.

"Kuzaku," he said.

"Hey."

"Setora."

"Yeah."

"Shihoru."

"...Right."

"Merry."

"Yes."

"Yume."

"Mew."

"Okay," Haruhiro said with relief.

Am I tired?

There's no point putting up a strong front. I'm tired. It's best to be aware of these things. But I can keep going.

How long do we have to keep walking? Until it's bright out? Will I last until then?

I should calculate, predict, and plan things out. It's difficult to make precise predictions. Even so, just flying by the seat of my pants is the worst thing I can do.

"Are we heading east, more or less...?" Haruhiro asked.

Yume told him, "Headin' northeast. Maybe a little more east than north, though?"

Whatever the case, we'll eventually end up setting foot in the mountains. It would be best to rest at least once before then. The odds are good that there are no vooloos around here. Let's rest. Should I say that now, in advance? It would be bad if we lost focus, so maybe I shouldn't say it until the time comes.

Unaaaaaaaaaaaaaaaaaaaoooooo!

There was a sudden cry that seemed to come from Kiichi, and Setora took off running.

It seemed some unforeseen situation had arisen.

Haruhiro reflexively shouted, "Setora, wait!" to stop her.

Setora didn't stop. She was already out of sight. He couldn't leave her be.

"Don't rush! Get ready, then move forward!"

Haruhiro drew his stiletto, passed Kuzaku, and chased after Setora. He soon realized there was something up ahead. He didn't so much see it as feel it. Initially, he thought there was a swell in the ground. Like it might be a small hill.

Gyaa! Gyaa! Gyaaaaaaa!

Kiichi was yowling. It was a frightening voice, like cats used when they were fighting.

The hill moved—or he got the sense that it had.

"Kiichi, get back!" Setora shouted.

"Haruhiro?! What is it?" Kuzaku caught up with him.

Haruhiro had come to a stop at some point. "I don't know, but—"

NNNNNNNNNNNNNNNNNNNNNNNNNNNNNNNN NNNNNNNNN...

A low, heavy sound like the earth rumbling was closing in on them. He had no idea what it was, but there was no doubt about it. Without any logic at all, he could say one thing with complete certainty. This thing was bad news.

"Whew! Ohhhh!" Yume had good eyes, so she might be able to see something surprising, unlike Haruhiro.

"Ma...!" was all Shihoru could get out. Was she trying to say something about magic?

"This is—"

There was something significant about the way Merry was speechless. Why did Haruhiro feel that was the case?

"I don't really know what it was," Kuzaku muttered. "But whatever world I came from before, there's no way it was like this. Seriously, Grimgar is such a—"

NNNNNNNNNNNNNNNNNNNNNNNNNNNNNNNN
NNNNNNNNNNNNNNNNNNNNNNNNNNNNNNNN
NNNNNNNNNNNNNNNNNNN...

It was here. What was coming? Haruhiro didn't know. How was he supposed to deal with it if he didn't know? He had no way of knowing that. But he had to do something about it. It was awful. He might not feel as strongly as Kuzaku, but he was sick of the way Grimgar did things like this to him. Sick of it or not, though, Haruhiro and the others were alive. They were living here. In Grimgar. The image of Merry, with her eyes closed, unmoving, flashed through his mind. It was enough to tear his heart to pieces. He never wanted to go through that again.

"Retreat!" Haruhiro backed away as he raised his voice. "Don't split up!"

NNNNNNNNNNNNNNNNNNNNNNNNNNNNNNNN
NNNNNNNNNNNNNNNNNNNNNNNNNNNNNNNN
NNNNNNNNNNNNNNNNNNNNNNNNNNNNNNNN
NNNNNNNNNNNNNNNNNNNNNNNNNNNNN...

What was it? Something was coming. That much was clear. What was coming? If he only had some clue...

"Dark...!" Shihoru summoned Dark the elemental.

Yume took a sharp breath, and fired an arrow. Did it hit? Or not?

NNNNNNNNNNNNNNNNNNNNNNNNNNNNNN
NNNNNNNNNNNNNNNNNNNNNNNNNNNNNNN...

Merry said something in a pained voice. It was probably "Sekaishu..." or something like that.

NNNNNNNNNNNNNNNNNNNNNNNNNNNNNN
NNNNNNNNNNNNNNNNN Sekaishu.

Was that a name? But why would Merry know its name? That didn't matter.

Haruhiro jumped back. He felt like something had touched the tips of his toes. No, he didn't just feel like it. Something had definitely touched him.

"It's coming from below!" Haruhiro shouted to warn the others.

NNNNNNNNNNNNNNNNNNNNNNNNNNNNN
Damn, I can't see. NNNNNNNNNNNNNNN *What is that?*
NNNNNNNNNNNNNNNN *But it keeps pressing in closer,*

that I can tell. NNNNNNNNNNNNNNN *I can feel it, keenly.* NNNNNNNNNNNNN *It's a thing, but at the same time not a thing.* NNNNNNNNNNN... *I feel like it's invading my heart.* NNNNNNNNNNNNNNNNNNNNNNNNN... *No, don't be led astray.*

He felt something brush the tip of his toes again. Haruhiro didn't jump back. He stomped it instead of running away. It wasn't hard. It wasn't soft, either. He could stomp it, but his foot sank in deep, and he felt like he might get pulled in.

In the end, Haruhiro tore his foot free and jumped back. Was that dangerous, just now? If he'd left his foot there, who knew what would have happened?

That said, it was a thing. No matter how crazy a thing it was, he could touch it. It had an actual physical form.

It touched the tips of his toes again. Haruhiro kicked it away.

"Don't be afraid! It's just—just some weird monster...!"

"Ahahaha!" Kuzaku laughed. "O Light, O Lumiaris, bestow the light of protection on my blade!"

He drew the sign of the hexagram with the point of his large katana, and it began to emit light. When Kuzaku swung his large katana, some black lumps were sent flying. They were like massive caterpillars.

"They're just caterpillars!" Haruhiro said, correcting himself from earlier. But he said it mostly to himself.

They were caterpillars. Mere caterpillars. They were caterpillars, so they were creepy. They might be poisonous, so he had to be careful, but there was no need to be unduly frightened.

NNNNNNNNNNNNNNNNNNNNNNNNNNNNNNNNN...

This NNNNNNNNNNNNNNNNNNNNNNNNNNNNNN...
What was it? It bothered him, but he wouldn't be able to figure it out even if he dwelt on it, so it was best not to worry about it. Haruhiro kicked the caterpillars that got close to him. Backing away a little at a time, he kicked, and kicked, and kicked away the caterpillars, which gave him an unpleasant sensation when he did.

Kuzaku didn't back away much. "Urrggghhhhh!" He made a big swing with his large katana to sweep away the caterpillars.

Yume was using her katana, too, it looked like.

Was Merry swinging around her head staff? What were Setora and Kiichi doing? He couldn't check.

Shihoru cried, "Go, Dark!" She was apparently sending out Dark.

It was questionable if the elemental had any effect.

Either way, this NNNNNNNNNNNNNNNNNNNNNNNN NNNNNNNNNNNNNNNNNNNNNNNNNNNN was irritating. It was like deep inside his ears, inside his head, a metal orb was vibrating. NNNNNNNNNNNNNNNNNNNNNNNNNNNNNNNN NNNNNNNNNNNNNNNNNNNNNNNNN It was a unique, low rumbling noise.

Right after he kicked the caterpillars for the umpteenth time, Haruhiro realized he had a nosebleed.

NNNNNNNNNNNNNNNNNNNNNNNNNNNNNNNNN NNNNN What could it be? Behind his eyes it felt hot—painful, even. NNNNNNNNNNNNNNNNNNNNNNNNNNNNNNNN

"Blaargh!" Kuzaku suddenly threw something up, his sword flashing as he nearly fell to his knees, cutting up more caterpillars. NNNNNNNNNNNNNNNNNNNNNNNN There were tears— no, these weren't tears. NNNNNNNNNNNNN Blood, there was blood coming out, from his eyes. NNNNNNNNNNNNN Haruhiro coughed. NNNNNNNNNNNNN He was dizzy. NNNNNNNN He was caught. NNNNNNNN His right leg. NNNN By the caterpillars. NNNNNN Haruhiro fell on his backside. NNNNNNN This NNNNNN was bad. NNNNN It felt awfully cold. NNNNN Like he'd lost NNNNNNN his right foot. NNNNNNN What was NNNNNN a Sekaishu? NNNN NNNNNNNNNNNNNNNNNNNNNNNNNNNNNNNNNN No, this was no good, no good, no good. NNNNN He kicked the caterpillars with his left foot, kicked, and kicked them away from his right foot, then crawled away and fled. He had to get away. It was going to swallow him up.

"Dark!" Shihoru called.

Dark let out a bizarre *vwoooooong* sound, and he shrunk down as he flew, and Haruhiro could see the arc of where he was going. Dark was going to slam into the main body of the caterpillars, or primary mass of them, the thing that was like a small hill made of caterpillars.

But all that happened was that the NNNNNNNNNNN NNNNNNNNNNNNNNNNNNNN noise grew stronger, and there was no other effect.

"Ohhhhhhhhhhhh!" Kuzaku was doing a good job fighting on his own, swinging his large katana this way and that, five or six meters ahead of Haruhiro, but he was in the process of being taken in by the caterpillars.

"No! We can't let this go on!" Merry was practically screaming. "Run! With everything you have! Get some distance from it! I'll...!"

What was Merry going to do? Why Merry? Casting aside his doubts, Haruhiro turned to go.

Kuzaku. Kuzaku was making no attempt to move. Had he not heard Merry's voice?

To Merry, Yume, Setora, anybody, he yelled, "Watch Shihoru!"

Protect her! I'm counting on you! Haruhiro thought as he rushed towards Kuzaku. He stepped on and over the caterpillars, brushing them away, opening a path.

"Kuzaku! Get back, Kuzaku!" he yelled.

Kuzaku turned towards him. "Ah! Sorry!"

"Hurry!"

"'Kay!"

Haruhiro ran as the caterpillars, a great number of them—no, was it better to say a great volume of them—rushed in from all over.

Kuzaku ran hard, too. If the caterpillars wrapped around him, that part of his body would go cold.

The NNNNNNNNNNNNNNNNNNNNNNNNNNNNNNN NNNNNNNN sound was getting stronger, too.

Haruhiro somehow beat the caterpillars off, shook them away, and ran for his life. The caterpillars were not advancing particularly quickly. That was his one salvation. That was why, though he didn't think for a moment that he could handle this situation, he felt like maybe he might be able to shake them off.

There was someone, probably Yume, who took his hand. Shihoru was probably beside them. Was Setora holding Kiichi? Also, Merry.

Merry.

Merry was...

"Delm, hel, en, saras, trem, rig, arve!"

"Oof?!"

"Doh?!"

The "oof" was probably Haruhiro, and the "doh" came from Kuzaku. Haruhiro and Kuzaku pitched forward at almost the same time as an intense blast of hot wind struck them from behind.

It was crazy hot. Rather than hot wind, it might have been more appropriate to call it a blast wave. Haruhiro narrowly managed to roll forward, but when he looked back before getting up properly, it burned his face. "Yeowch!"

No, it might not have burned him, but the heat felt painful enough to make him think he had maybe gotten a little singed. It was far too large to call it a pillar of flame. There was a wall, no, a cliff of flame rising before him.

Magic.

This had to be Arve Magic.

But it wasn't Shihoru's magic. Shihoru only used Dark these days. Besides, Shihoru hadn't acquired a single Arve Magic spell.

"Ouch, ouch, ouch, ouch, ouch!" Kuzaku cried as he crawled forward at an impressive speed.

Haruhiro stood up. It was hot. There were sparks flying off the cliff of flames. It was more than just hot.

Haruhiro sheathed his stiletto, covered his face with his hands, and stumbled towards his comrades.

Shihoru was cowering as she stared at the cliff of flames. She seemed a little out of it.

A few words slipped from Shihoru's mouth. "Blaze Cliff."

That had to be the name of a spell. But Shihoru wasn't the one who'd used that Arve Magic.

Yume looked at Merry, who was beside her. She immediately averted her gaze.

"I..." Merry looked down, pressing her left hand to her forehead. "I... Sekaishu. Removal. With just this. I can't. So I. Magic. I...used magic. While I still can. I—"

Setora was holding Kiichi. Crouching down, she set the gray nyaa down on the ground. "Priest. What is Sekaishu?"

"Sekai...shu." Merry mumbled. "I..."

I don't know, she continued in a mumble that trailed off and vanished.

Haruhiro stood there dumbfounded. There was practically nothing he could do.

I don't know. That's what Merry had said.

Sekaishu. Even after she had clearly spoken that unfamiliar word, Merry had used magic. Using Blaze Cliff. Arve Magic. This was likely the second time they'd seen that spell used. The first time had been in the village, with Jessie.

Merry didn't know it. Light magic was one thing, but a priest like Merry couldn't use Arve Magic.

"We have to run, while we still can." Haruhiro made every effort to make sure his voice didn't quiver. Then, walking over to Merry, he extended his right hand to her.

Do I have the resolve? he wondered. *I will recognize it all. I'll take it in, and accept it.*

"Let's go, Merry."

Merry raised her face. He didn't intend to wait for her to nod. Haruhiro took Merry's hand.

Yeah, of course. I have the resolve.

Haruhiro took Merry's hand and started walking. First, they had to get away from the Blaze Cliff. He didn't know what Sekaishu—or whatever it was—was, but they'd run away from that nonsensical monster. Then they'd head east.

If they went east, they should come to the sea.

If they could reach the sea, they'd manage somehow.

Grimgar
of
Fantasy and Ash

HOW DID YOU like it? Volume 11 of *Grimgar of Fantasy and Ash*?

It's already Volume 11. Or is it only Volume 11?

For my part, I've cleared the first hurdle—that is to say the part I had to get past no matter what—so I'm a little relieved.

No, maybe not. There's still a way to go.

To tell you the truth, originally Haruhiro and the others should have been back in Alterna by now, or close to Alterna, at least. But for some reason it didn't go that way, and thanks to that, it looks like our fun little excursion will continue a little longer.

Honestly, I'm exhausted after completing this manuscript, but I'd like you to let me say just one thing.

I think the next volume will surely be a cheery, fun, fluffy adventure story.

To my editor, Harada-san, to Eiri Shirai-san, to the designers of KOMEWORKS among others, to everyone involved in production and sales of this book, and finally to all of you people now holding this book, I offer my heartfelt appreciation and all of my love. Now, I lay down my pen for today.

I hope we will meet again.

—Ao Jyumonji

Experience these great light**novel** titles from Seven Seas Entertainment

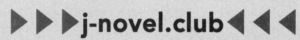